SING S

An Autumn Jade Mystery

BY
STEVE WHAN

MEIGAN,
I hope you like
horses and unicorns!
SW

Autumn Jade Publishing
Vancouver

SING SONG GIRLS
Autumn Jade Publishing

This novel is a work of fiction. Any references to historical events; to real people, living or dead; or to real locales are intended only to give the fiction a sense of reality and authenticity. Other names, characters, places, and incidents either are the product of the author's imagination or are used fictitiously, and their resemblance, if any, to real-life counterparts is entirely coincidental. Autumn Jade Publishing and the author disclaim any responsibility or liability for any personal injuries sustained by anyone as a result of the practice of any of the techniques illustrated or discussed in this book.

ISBN 0-9688198-2-6

Published in Canada by Autumn Jade Publishing, Vancouver. Web Site: http://www.autumnjade.com

Printed in Canada
Cover Art by Trevor Lai

Teachers open the doors, but you must enter by yourself – Chinese Proverb

This book is dedicated to my parents, who helped me find the door, and to my grade four English teacher, Ms. Horne, who opened it for me. Thanks!

FOREWORD

Having previously read *Bullets on the Bund* and *The Emperor's Pendant,* I am happy to encourage Steven to continue to write more children's mysteries. *Sing Song Girls* is another splendid children's novel now available for children in the Middle Childhood Years to read for themselves. These are those years when children need strong, charismatic heroes and heroines, and Steven Whan's books deliver them.

It is uncommon, but wonderful to see a book character portrayed who is of Asian heritage and joined her family through adoption, paired with characters who lived in the country of her ancestry long ago. Imaginative, fun, chock full of skillfully researched history in China, but most-wonderful-of-all, Steven Whan's offer children born and adopted in China a heroine who is much like themselves to inspire their imagination and dreams. Yet the books are also of great value to many other readers: all children of Asian ancestry and most especially those whose families originated in China; plus all children whose interest is captivated by the intrigues contained in a good mystery.

I'm so honored to have been asked by Steven and his delightful family to provide readers — new and old — to enter the world of his charming characters in his new children's mystery. I hope you will relish the adventures just as my children and I have!

Jane Brown, M.S.W.

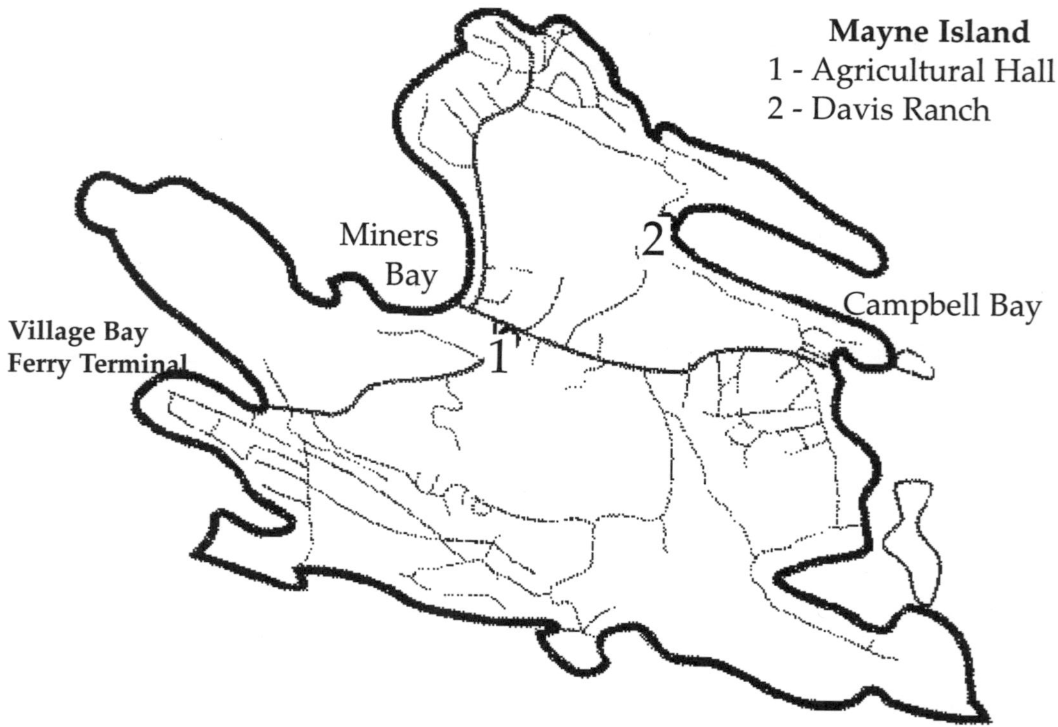
Mayne Island
1 - Agricultural Hall
2 - Davis Ranch
Miners Bay
Campbell Bay
Village Bay Ferry Terminal
1
2

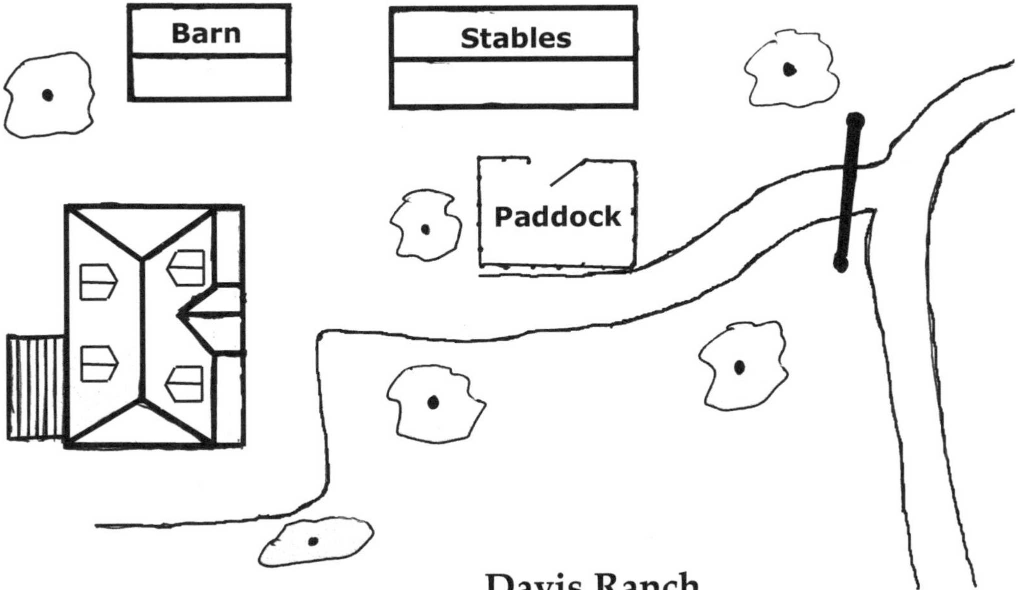

Davis Ranch

秋玉

1

The roar of thundering hooves reverberated within Autumn's soul. Her black, shoulder length hair swirled around in wild disarray as her horse streaked through the forest.

"Good girl!" Autumn whispered to Moonbeam, gently stroking her silky mane. The mare responded by lightly leaping a small creek and dodging several low-hanging branches.

The year was 1142. Autumn and her magnificent horse were on a mission. She had a message from the Emperor to deliver to General Yue Fei, whose northern expedition force was winning battle after battle against the rebellious enemy soldiers of the Jin.

Though the General's camp was more than a day's ride away, Autumn had promised to deliver the Emperor's message before sunset. She hoped she would not be too late. "Faster, Moonbeam! Fly like the wind."

They had already covered more than half of the distance to the front lines. Moonbeam had a smile on her finely sculpted equine face. If horses could talk, would she be saying: Autumn, thank you for allowing my spirit to run free?

Moonbeam was by far the most powerful horse in the kingdom

and Autumn was honoured to ride her. Autumn allowed herself a brief moment to relive the scene of her departure. The Emperor's words would be forever etched on her mind. "The fate of our country rests with these twelve brave heroes," he had solemnly proclaimed.

"I won't let you, or the people, down," Autumn had promised.

The other eleven riders had been left behind many hours ago. Autumn pulled out her map and checked for the landmarks she needed to follow. A diamond-shaped peak was her next goal. Ah, there it was, straight ahead. A fast-moving river was suddenly in front of them. Moonbeam hit the water and barrelled through, never slowing her pace.

"That's my girl," Autumn breathed into Moonbeam's right ear.

The icy waters poured into Autumn's soft leather riding boots and quickly froze her feet. Moonbeam's powerful legs found traction on the sandy riverbed and out of the water they leapt. Autumn spotted the narrow pass they had to use to get over the mountains. She gently steered Moonbeam in the right direction using light tapping movements with her feet.

As they sped through the pass, small rocks tumbled down from the unstable slope above her. Something sharp struck Autumn on the right arm and she winced in pain. She wrapped the reins tightly in her left hand and calmed her breathing so she could ignore the burning sensation in her right biceps.

Moonbeam launched herself out of the mountain pass like a forcefully discharged cannonball and they scrambled down the winding trail to the forest below.

"Slowww!" Autumn commanded several minutes later. The trees in the forest were denser here, almost like a wall.

The forest parted in front of them and Autumn found herself entering a moss-covered glen. Moonbeam's ears perked up, and

Autumn pulled sharply on the reins to stop her.

"What is it, girl?" Autumn asked. The hushed silence of the clearing was unnerving.

There was a small emerald green pool of water in the middle of the glen. Autumn gently coaxed the horse towards it.

Moonbeam looked nervously back and forth as she leaned over to drink from the pond. Autumn pulled out her flask to do the same.

There was a slight shimmering in the air and suddenly an animal appeared. It floated gracefully over the pond.

Moonbeam peered anxiously back at Autumn. "It's okay, Moonbeam," she whispered softly, entranced by the quiet majesty of the beast before her.

It had the body of a goat with the shaggy tail of an ox. Its underbelly was yellowish and the rest of its body was multicoloured, having five of the most gay and perfect colours: red, yellow, blue, white, and black.

It was a *zhi,* the legendary Chinese unicorn, the most auspicious of all the animals. Zhi were often associated with the delivery of premonitions that would soon come true.

Autumn finally found her nerve. "My name is Autumn Jade and this is my horse Moonbeam. I'm sorry if we've disturbed you."

The zhi looked directly into her eyes. The voice Autumn heard within her own mind was sweet and delicate, like the ringing of a small silver bell.

"One will die so another may live. Remember, a messenger is only as truthful as the one who creates the message . . . "

"But what do you mean?" Autumn began, but the air was shimmering again. The zhi disappeared as quickly as it had come. The sounds of chirping birds and buzzing insects suddenly filled the air.

"Let's get out of here!"

Moonbeam required no further urging. Her pounding hooves chewed up the moss as she charged headlong through the forest.

"Almost there, it's just a little further," Autumn sighed. She could see signs of the General's army on the other side of the valley. One last hard push and they'd be there!

The final hour was a weary blur. Autumn was finding it difficult to ignore the growing pain in her upper arm. After what seemed like an eternity, she pulled up as the rear sentries challenged her approach.

"The eagle flies over the kingdom!" Autumn shouted out the Emperor's pass code. "I carry an urgent message for General Yue Fei."

Moonbeam walked quietly through the encampment, a light sweat glistening on her spotted coat. Soldiers looked up from where they were resting to observe the magnificent animal and her beautiful rider. Autumn quickly found her way to the General's tent.

She dismounted and hugged Moonbeam's broad chest. "You're the best horse a girl could ever have hoped for," she said. Autumn passed through the front flaps of the tent and waited to hand the message cylinder to the General.

The General nodded for Autumn to approach. He unrolled the scroll and began cursing. The message was an edict from the Emperor ordering the General to avoid the decisive battle and withdraw to the South. The General stared long and hard at Autumn. This was the same man who was said to have defeated an enemy 500,000 strong with only 800 soldiers. Autumn suddenly saw that her message was not what the General wanted to hear.

"I judge you to be an innocent pawn in all of this." The General dropped the scroll and crushed it under his boot heel. "I will be ignoring the Emperor's wishes in this matter. It would appear that the treacherous Emperor and his jealous Prime Minister want my head on a pole, but I'm not going to make it quite so easy for them. I plan on winning this final battle as a gift to the Chinese people. You may go."

A shocked Autumn quickly left the tent. The zhi's message suddenly made sense to her. If the General was correct, he was an unwitting victim of political treachery, and Autumn's valiant ride had been for nothing. The pain in her right arm was almost too much to bear. Autumn decided to look after Moonbeam and then tend to herself. They both had a well-deserved rest coming, even if her journey had been pointless.

* * *

I awoke from a sound sleep, the remnants of the dream still fresh in my mind. "Ouch!" I cried out. My Australian Shepherd dog, Watson, was still enthralled in his own dream world. One of his hind toe nails was digging into my right arm. That explained part of my dream, anyway!

Over the course of the summer, my vivid dreams of a baby abandoned on the docks of old Shanghai had gradually been replaced by epic stories of battles from long ago and other dreams about China's magnificent history.

I'd been doing a lot of reading while my leg was mending, most recently about how Emperor Gaozong had sent his General twelve orders to stop the war within a single day. General Yue Fei had no alternative but to obey or else be charged with insubordination. Unfortunately for him, Emperor Gaozong and his Prime Minister had already surrendered to the Jin. They falsely accused the General of treachery. At the age of 39, General Yue Fei was executed while in prison. Not really a cheerful story to be dreaming about!

I rubbed Watson's exposed belly. "Come on, you big lump, time to get up. We have a lot to do today."

My friend Vanessa and I were leaving the next day for two weeks on Mayne Island. We were helping out at a real horse ranch! I quickly dressed, took care of Watson's toe nails, and then headed down for breakfast.

秋玉

2

Dad was sitting at the kitchen table intent on a small silver object that he held in one hand. I poured out a bowl of cereal and grabbed a glass from the cupboard for juice. I sat down beside Dad to get a better look.

"Whatcha playing with?" I asked.

"It's just a little something I picked up for your trip. I thought you might want to check your email while you're gone." Dad knew I couldn't go long without accessing Sisters of China or the other services I belonged to. I was just like him when it came to computers.

"With that? How?"

"It's the latest in wireless handheld computers. I read in the news last week that Mayne Island has just put in a wireless network that covers the entire island. This little marvel will automatically connect up to their network and let you access the Internet. You'll be able to retrieve your email, chat with your friends and continue with your Shanghai research."

My father was a whiz when it came to computers, but this was too much. "It's cute, but where's the keyboard? I've tried those little chiclet keys before. Nobody has fingers small enough to use them."

Dad suppressed a grin. He placed the unit into a stand on the table and pressed a tiny red button.

"Wow!" I exclaimed. "No way."

"Impressive, isn't it," laughed Dad.

The glowing red outline of a keyboard had suddenly appeared on the tabletop.

"Want to try it out? There's a sensor that monitors the reflection of the infrared light being projected. It can tell which 'keys' you are trying to strike by the way the reflection changes. I've loaded up some basic software already. You have to promise that you'll give me your feedback on it. I need to write a report for my boss once you get back." Dad got up from the table. "I have to get ready for work, I hope you enjoy it."

"Thanks, Dad. This has a mega-cool factor. I can hardly wait to show it to Adam."

Mom came out of her office at the sound of Adam's name.

"Morning, Mom," I said as she entered the kitchen.

"Hi, honey." She pointed out the window to the house next door. "Do you have any idea what Adam is up to? He just crossed over to his parent's garage dressed in a lab coat, rubber gloves and an old gas mask."

Adam was the handsomest guy around — at least I thought so. He lived next door and was usually my partner in our adventures. Lately, though, he'd become somewhat of a recluse.

"I haven't the slightest," I tried to sound nonchalant. Actually, he'd been keeping whatever he was up to a big secret and I was getting really annoyed with him. I was ready to give him the stinky-eye, as Mrs. Lee would say, but he hadn't even dropped by in the past two weeks to see how my recuperation was going. "I don't think Mr. and Mrs. B. really know what he's up to either!"

About halfway through our summer vacation Adam had found something at the beach. Ever since then he'd squirreled himself away in the garage trying to finish a mysterious project before school started up again. It hadn't bothered me at first because Mrs. Lee was still staying with us and she'd been teaching me all sorts of amazing martial arts techniques. But since Mrs. Lee had left us to help nursemaid an old friend in Taiwan, I'd suddenly realized that Adam hadn't been coming over all the time like he used to. It was especially annoying from someone I considered my best friend — if not more.

The telephone rang and Mom picked up the handset. "Hello, Ethnicity Clothing Designs, how may I help you? Oh, hi Vanessa. Autumn's right here."

I jumped up and took the phone from Mom's outstretched arm.

"All packed?" I asked Vanessa.

"Almost, but it's been difficult trying to stuff everything I want to bring onto my poor bicycle. Couldn't we just get our parents to drive us to the ranch?"

"Nah, it'll be more fun if we don't have to rely on our parents to get us to Mayne Island. And my leg needs the exercise. What are you bringing, anyway?"

"My hair dryer, make-up kit, you know, stuff like that."

"What for? We're working at a horse ranch, not a beauty parlour or a health spa!"

"Yeah, I know that, but we might meet some cute boys and I want to look good. And what about you, still bringing a computer?"

"Dad just gave me something special to bring instead of my heavy old laptop. Besides, I'm sure Mrs. Davis has a hair dryer you can borrow. It's more important that you bring the costume and other things we talked about. We're only gone for two weeks, you know."

"No problem, most everything is already packed. Really. I was just hoping to bring some little extras with me. Have you talked to Adam recently?"

I stood up to peer out the window.

"He's still working on his project. Mom saw him all dressed up like a mad scientist this morning. I really don't know what's gotten into him. He's been ignoring everyone lately."

"Did you tell him about our trip?"

"Yes. I told him that Mr. Davis had invited all three of us to stay for the next two weeks at his ranch. Adam said he hoped to join us later in the week and he would bring a big surprise with him. Are you going to be ready to leave by nine-thirty tomorrow morning? The ferry leaves for the Gulf Islands at ten twenty-five. That will give us plenty of time to cycle to the terminal."

"Sure, I'll meet you at the end of your street. See you tomorrow, Autumn."

"*Zaijian,* Vanessa."

Mom was standing in the doorway to her office. "I almost forgot. I was telling Mrs. Chandler about your trip. She asked if you could drop by her place after dinner."

"Thanks, Mom. I will!" Mrs. Chandler always had great stories to share about her experiences. After her husband had died many years ago, she had decided to live life to the fullest. "I think I'll call Vanessa back and see if she wants to come along, too."

秋玉

3

Vanessa was coming up the road as I opened the door. "Ready?" she called out.

"Yep! Let's go."

Mrs. Chandler's house was at the end of the street. She was out in her front yard. Her strawberry blonde hair bobbed wildly as she briskly pushed a hand mower back and forth across her lawn.

"Hi, girls, I'll be done in a minute. Head around back and make yourselves at home."

Mrs. Chandler, as seemed her usual habit, had set out lemonade and cookies for us.

"Autumn, how's the stick fighting coming along?" she asked, putting the lawnmower away.

"Okay, I guess," I replied. I was trying to be more humble about my skills per Mrs. Lee's instructions.

"Ready to do some sparring with me?"

"You'd probably whomp me. Maybe when I get back. Mrs. Lee said I have the speed and stamina but an unfortunate lack of experience. She also said something about needing a bag of sneaky tricks."

"We'll see, we'll see. You will only get better by practising with someone who challenges your skills. So, what can I help you two ladies with this time?" she said with a mischievous twinkle in her eye.

"We're going to stay at a horse ranch and . . . "

"Horses," Mrs. Chandler burst out, "have I got some stories to tell you. Wild stallions, race horses, or riding tips — what's your pleasure?"

"Wild stallions!" blurted out Vanessa. "Well," she said looking at me, "it sure sounds exciting."

Mrs. Chandler chuckled. "That was one of my favourite vacations. About ten years ago I was offered a chance to ride with the wild stallions of Wyoming. Every year they cull the herd and sell off the extra horses. They're always looking for experienced riders to help out. Anyway, the ranch had a horse whisperer whose job it was to get the horses to the point where they would accept a rider."

"What's a horse whisperer?" I giggled, imagining a grown man running around a field whispering into horses' ears.

Vanessa waved her hand in the air, "I know! It's a person who communicates with horses in a special way."

"It's much more than that, Vanessa. Horses have their own language that they use to communicate with each other. It is a very soft language, very subtle — almost a whisper. A whisperer speaks to the horse in the horse's own language rather than trying to teach him ours. Because horses are nonverbal, they use their bodies to speak. The twitch of an ear, the movement of an eye, the carriage of the tail, and the way a horse carries himself in your presence all have meaning. Long ago, horse whispering was practised by Indian Shamans and those said to have mystical powers over animals."

"Is it hard to do?" I asked.

"Well, the cowboys on the ranch made it look easy. Hmmm, I have an album in the house that will help explain it better." She stood up. "Be right back. It'll just take me a minute to find it."

"She's so cool," commented Vanessa once Mrs. Chandler was out of sight.

"I know. I hope my life is one tenth as interesting as hers has been!"

"Life is as interesting as you want to make it," said Mrs. Chandler from behind me. "I started this scrapbook several years ago to share my trips with my grandchildren."

Mrs. Chandler opened a thick album full of photographs surrounded by colourful trim and special calligraphy. It made a dull thud as the two covers hit the tabletop.

"I'll give you a moment to read the captions." She pointed at one of the pictures. "The cowboy's name was Thomas. Here in this first picture, Thomas was chasing the horse around the paddock. He was waiting for the stallion to turn and face him."

"Why?" asked Vanessa.

"He needed to grab the horse's attention and keep it. See, in this next photo, once the horse was looking at him he used subtle shifts of body language to keep the horse focused on him."

I couldn't make out the next series of pictures. They all looked the same to me. "What's going on here?"

"I don't even know why I kept so many of those ones. Thomas was doing this little dance with the horse. He'd step then stop, step then stop. The trick was to fool the horse into turning his hindquarters away. Then, quick as lightening, he looped a rope over the horse's head."

"I bet the horse didn't like that," said Vanessa.

"A funny thing, the horse actually turned to Thomas for

reassurance that everything was okay." Mrs. Chandler turned the page. "This is my favourite picture. The horse is smelling a human up close for the first time. He actually touched his nose to the back of Thomas' hand."

My body quivered. "I've got goose bumps."

"Me, too," agreed Vanessa. "This is great!"

"After that, it got easier. Thomas would apply a little tension in the rope and watch for a change on the horse's face. Half an hour after that first touch, and he was putting a saddle on the horse."

In the next photograph the horse was bucking into the air.

"Whoa, guess he didn't like that!" laughed Vanessa.

"You can't blame him. The back is the most vulnerable place for a horse. It's usually where they'd be attacked by a predator. Thomas calmed him down and left the saddle on for a few more hours. By the next day he was riding him."

"That's amazing, and all without hurting the horse," I said.

"Horses will work their hearts out for us. Especially if they learn early on to trust humans and we present the training material in a way they understand. That's what horse whisperers do. It's not just a way of working with a horse. It's also the most natural way to treat them."

Mrs. Chandler closed the album. "Anything else you want to know about?"

"What's that beeping sound I keep hearing?" asked Vanessa.

"Oh, my silly computer is just trying to get my attention. Around this time of the evening I usually spend time chatting online with some of my old school chums. The Internet has made it so easy for us to stay in touch. We set up a private chat room and get together twice a week to just plain gossip. We can spend hours talking about the silliest things."

"I know what you're saying!" I chuckled. "The SoC, sorry, I

mean the Sisters of China, recently set up a chat room system for its members. It's great, but like you say, we can easily blather away a whole evening."

Vanessa looked puzzled. "I have no idea what you two are talking about. We don't even have email at home. My parents are very old-fashioned when it comes to computers and the Internet."

"Don't worry, Vanessa, I'll bring you up to speed. My Dad is lending me a great little handheld computer for our trip. Thanks as always for the visit, Mrs. Chandler. We should let you get to your friends."

"Yes," agreed Vanessa, "thanks for telling us about horse whisperers. I'm going to get my Mom to drive me to the library before it closes so I can learn more about them."

"Take care, girls. Let me know if there is anything else I can do to help out. Enjoy your trip!"

秋玉

4

Qiu Yu glanced over the top of her dime novel. Auntie Shu-Shu was fussing about the room and had dropped several books on the floor.

Auntie Shu-Shu had been Qiu Yu's guardian since her parents had been killed. Auntie had always been very strict with her rebellious niece, but became even more so once Qiu Yu became her direct responsibility. Their relationship was reaching a breaking point now that Qiu Yu towered over her diminutive aunt.

"Please, Auntie, can't you sit still? Why are you wandering all over the house?"

Qiu Yu thought for sure that Auntie Shu-Shu would rip into her again for poor manners or poor posture, but her aunt just stopped and abruptly sat down on the edge of the sofa.

"What is it, Auntie?"

"Child, you have no idea, do you?" Auntie Shu-Shu raised her skirt to expose her tiny feet in dainty silk shoes. They were no larger than two apples attached to the ends of her legs. "Can you even guess at the pain I endure every day because of these?"

Qiu Yu was taken aback by Auntie's sudden candour. "No . . . "

"When I was five, my feet were broken and bound. I used to love exploring and playing just like you do. That was all taken away from me the day the foot-binder came to the house. My mother didn't do a thing to stop it. I've spent my whole life fighting the never-ending agony that my feet cause me. Every night I soak them, hoping the terrible ache will momentarily go away. But there is no point, is there?" Auntie Shu-Shu sighed. "What use are Lotus Petals when you are too old to get married?"

"Oh, Auntie, I'm so sorry."

"Consider yourself lucky. Your father and his wife, may the souls of the faithfully departed rest in peace, didn't have to make that decision for you. And do you know what? The whole thing seems so pointless now that the practice has been outlawed."

Auntie Shu-Shu hiccupped, then let out a guffaw. Her belly began to shake and then laughter exploded from deep inside her. "Ha, ha, ha, ho, ho."

Tears rolled down her face. She gripped her sides to contain the uncontrollable laughter.

"Auntie, are you all right? I've never seen you like this before."

Auntie Shu-Shu finally began to calm down. "The gem cannot be polished without friction, and man cannot be perfected without trials. After fifty years of suffering I deserved to laugh again." She smiled. "Now go, go play with your friends."

Qiu Yu gave her Aunt a fierce hug. "When I get back tonight, can we talk? I want to learn all about your life. Maybe this can be a fresh start for us?"

"Yes, child, yes it may."

Amy was waiting at the British Consulate for her friends, Soo-Lin and Qiu Yu. She had arranged for two extra bicycles. Qiu Yu and Soo-Lin hopped on the borrowed bikes and they all started cycling down Foochow Road.

"Where are you taking us?" Soo-Lin shouted to Amy.

"It's a surprise!" laughed Amy. "Just trust me and try to keep up."

After several minutes of dodging rickshaws and careless pedestrians, Amy jumped off her bike and walked it through an elaborate doorway into a narrow alleyway called Hui Le Li, or Seeking Happiness Lane.

"In there?" Soo-Lin whispered to Qiu Yu. "I've heard about this alley, only sing-song girls and prostitutes live here."

"Amy said to trust her, and I do," replied Qiu Yu. "Are you coming or not?"

There was a narrow slit between two buildings, a gap for a concrete sidewalk less than a metre wide. It turned a sharp angle and then suddenly widened. Openings for darkened cellars extended well into the alleyway — with no guardrails — just a hole with steps that you could easily fall down. Tenements full of poor Chinese were on one side. The back walls of stores and other businesses were on the other.

A door opened and a wizened old man tossed out a bucketful of foul liquid. It slowly oozed its way down the opposite wall onto a rat-infested pile of debris.

Qiu Yu gagged. "I hope this will be worth it."

Amy knocked on an ornate red door set into the bricks of the alley wall. It opened silently on well-oiled hinges and a pale hand beckoned the girls to enter.

Once inside, the girls couldn't believe their eyes. The bleak alley was in stark contrast to the simple charm of the courtyard. There was a small Buddhist altar beside a hand-carved meditation bench. Incense sticks released the sweet aroma of jasmine to mask errant smells that wafted over the courtyard wall. Cheerful red lanterns and gold-lettered banners hung from the beams of the house.

"Soo-Lin, Qiu Yu, I'd like to introduce you to Sorrow. She's a very popular sing-song girl here in Shanghai. I met her last night at a party my Dad gave for new staff at the British Consulate."

Sorrow smiled shyly at the girls as they bowed to her.

"Thank you, Amy," Sorrow sang in a lilting voice. "I hope you can help me with my, er, little problem."

"Could you please repeat for my friends what you told me after the party?" Amy prompted.

"It's difficult to explain," Sorrow began. "Last week I was performing at the Great World. During a break I went up to the sixth floor. There had been a rumour going around that there was a unicorn and for a few coins you could get a prediction of your future."

"Don't tell me you paid them good money! Unicorns are mythical animals," snickered Qiu Yu in disbelief.

"Well, I thought so, too. But I stood in line, paid my money and what I saw looked the same as the unicorns I heard about when I was a child."

"What about its prediction?" asked Soo-Lin. "You can't tell me that was for real."

"Here's where it starts getting strange. I had a vision while I was with the unicorn. Although I never heard it speak, images began to form in my mind. I saw myself finding a baby abandoned at the Shanghai racetrack. But I wasn't alone when I found the baby; there was a girl with red hair and a British accent. I was very surprised when I later saw Amy at the party! I didn't realize it until now, but the two of you were also in the vision. I can honestly claim I haven't met either of you before."

"Tell them the rest," urged Amy.

"The final images were of me holding onto the baby and placing a bet on the third race. The money I won allowed me to buy my freedom and escape to Nanjing with my new baby. I'm asking for your help to prove the unicorn's prediction. I want the vision to come true with all my heart."

"Sorrow, can we come with you tonight?" asked Amy. "Maybe we can discover what's going on."

"That would be wonderful," bowed Sorrow. "I'm starting at the Great World at seven o'clock. Meet me back here at six-thirty — you can follow along behind my sedan chair."

秋玉

5

Watson was sitting in the middle of my stuff. I had already eaten breakfast and was going over my packing list one more time.

"Sorry, boy. You can't come with us this time."

He put out his left paw and made a Lassie-like whimper.

"I wish I could bring you," I apologized, "but Mr. Davis said he was worried about you being around their pregnant horse."

Watson gave me his best "who me?" look and rolled onto his back to expose his white underbelly. He waved his right front paw in the air to get my attention.

"Nice try, but I've got to go. I'll see you in two weeks. Please be good while I'm gone. You better listen to Mom and Dad or else, do you hear me?"

I gave Watson one last hug and grabbed my gear.

"All set, Autumn?" asked Mom.

"I think so," I replied. "If I've forgotten anything, I'll give you a call. Hopefully Adam will be coming before the end of the week like he promised. He should have some extra room on his bike if I need anything special."

After hugging Mom I took my things outside. I attached the

panniers to the racks on my bicycle, strapped my walking stick to the cross bar and pressed each tire with my thumb to check the air pressure.

"Leaving without saying goodbye?" Adam called over the fence separating our two backyards. He parted two boards and stepped through. The rubber gloves and gas mask were gone, but he still had on a grease-covered lab coat and heavy rubber boots.

"I'm meeting Vanessa in ten minutes." I stared at his garb. "I'm not too happy with you right now. I've always shared everything, and you won't even give me a hint about your little project! Am I your best friend or not?"

"I'm almost ready," he grinned sheepishly. "If everything works out, I'll see you later this week."

Adam could be so irritating. "And if it doesn't?"

"Don't worry, I think I got it right this time."

"It?"

He laughed and squeezed my hand. "Have a great trip. See you in a couple of days."

"Zaijian, Adam, I'll try to miss you."

I hopped on my bike. It wobbled a bit as I adjusted to riding with about forty extra pounds of gear hanging off the rear rack. My left leg was not quite working at one hundred percent yet. The rehabilitation process had taken a lot longer than I'd expected.

Vanessa waved at me from the entrance to Pebble Hill Park. "What's the stick for? You aren't really limping anymore."

I leaned my bike against a tree and pulled out the walking stick. I checked to make sure we were alone. I took up a fighting stance and swung the stick around in a figure eight. I snapped the stick out at the tree and took a quarter inch thick branch cleanly off.

Vanessa covered her mouth in surprise. "Oh. My. Gosh. Is that one of the moves Mrs. Lee taught you?"

"Mrs. Lee can break off a branch twice that thick. Remember those bad guys in the tunnel? If I'd had this walking stick and had known what Mrs. Lee taught me this summer, we would have had a chance of defending ourselves."

"You just have to show me how to do that!"

"I asked Mrs. Lee about that, but she feels I need fighting experience first. 'You can't teach others what you don't fully understand yourself' was what she said. I'll arrange with Mrs. Chandler to do some sparring practise when we get back, then we'll see."

Vanessa was pouting.

"Well, I suppose I could show you the basics. Once we get to the ranch, okay?"

Vanessa and I whisked down Englishman's Bluff road to the ferry causeway. Thirty minutes later we'd paid our fares and were sitting at the ramp waiting for the *M.V. Queen of Tsawwassen* to depart.

A strong wind came up as we crossed the Straight of Georgia. The big ferry swayed from side to side as it plowed through the wind and rough ocean water.

Vanessa was looking a little green.

"Feeling all right?" I asked.

"I'm beginning to wish I hadn't had such a big breakfast."

We were sitting on the top deck of the ship. "Let's go down a level," I recommended. "The motion is not usually as bad there."

Vanessa suppressed a belch. "Thanks."

The movement of the ship was less noticeable on the main deck.

"I guess you're not a big fan of roller coaster rides," I laughed.

"We went to Disneyland a few years ago. I got sick on the first ride. After that my parents only let me ride the slow kiddie rides. It was really embarrassing."

Since Vanessa wasn't being much company — I mean, who would be when they were feeling all green and barfy — I pulled out some rope and a jawbreaker-sized lead ball from my pack.

Vanessa's eyes went wide. "What's that for?"

"I'm making a slungshot."

"You mean a slingshot, right?"

"No, slungshot with a 'u'. Just watch. First I loop the rope over my hand four times, like this."

I wound the rope around my opened hand.

"Then I feed it around and through my fingers four times."

I carefully slipped in the lead ball.

"Now four more times in this direction. The knot I've just made is called a monkey-fist knot."

"Is that ever cool. What can you do with it?"

"Sailors used to make them to help throw a line to shore. Mrs. Lee showed me how to use it as a weapon to protect myself. Let me finish it off and then you can try it out."

I braided a third piece of rope into the tails coming off the monkey-fist knot. I wrapped both ends and made a handle.

I passed the finished slungshot to Vanessa. "Bounce the end lightly on your thigh to see how it feels."

Vanessa swung the monkey-fist encased lead ball into her leg. "Ouch!" she winced. "Oh man, that smarts! That Mrs. Lee is something else. You should have warned me. I think I already have a bruise."

"I did say bounce it lightly, not swing it."

"Can I make one?"

I pulled out another piece of rope and passed it to her. Vanessa's attempts to tie the knot helped distract her from the ship's rolling passage across the straight.

Vanessa had noticeably relaxed as we entered Active Pass and the swaying of the boat calmed down.

"Whew," Vanessa sighed, "I'm glad that's over with."

At Sturdies Bay on Galiano Island there was a brief but intense flurry of activity as half the passengers disembarked. In less than ten minutes we were heading across Active Pass to Mayne Island.

"When were you born?" I asked.

"Huh?"

"What date were you born? I want to see if you have an auspicious horoscope for our trip."

"My birth date is April 17, 1991. I'm an Aries, if that helps."

"Chinese astrology works differently than the signs of the zodiac. It's called the Stem-Branch system." I pulled out a small book I'd recently bought on the subject.

"1991 was the year of the White Sheep. April 17 makes you a Red Snake. What time were you born?"

"That matters, too?"

"According to this book it does."

"Around two-thirty in the morning."

"Okay, it says here that your lucky element is wood, your lucky colour is green and you will have even better luck if your name has an 'A' sound in it."

"Hey, that's neat. I love to wear green and I have a lucky name! What about you?"

I was just about to tell her when the public address system came to life. "Your attention please," announced a recorded voice, "we are now arriving at Village Bay on Mayne Island. All passengers disembarking please return to the car deck."

"Let's go!" I clapped the book shut. "I'll tell you my Chinese horoscope once we're on our way."

We raced down the stairs to the vehicle deck and unlocked our bikes.

"Do you think we'll get to ride the horses?" Vanessa asked.

"I hope so. When I talked to Mr. Davis he didn't mention it, but I'm sure if we ask him he won't say no."

秋玉

6

The big doors swung open and we were immediately reminded of the monster hill leading away from the dock.

"I think there's too much weight on our bikes," Vanessa groaned.

"Let's wait for all of the cars to leave and then push our way up to the main road," I suggested.

We were perspiring by the time we reached the road.

"Right or left?" Vanessa asked.

"Do you want fast or scenic?"

"How about the route that has the fewest hills?"

"Sorry, Vanessa, but this is an island. You go up, you go down, you go up and you go down." I pulled out a map of Mayne Island. "We could do like last time and take Village Bay Road to Miners Bay. After this little uphill bit, we take Campbell Bay Road and we're there."

"Fine by me," said Vanessa.

"And since we're not chasing after bad guys we don't have to hurry. Lead on. You can set the pace."

The early morning chill had burned off and we were sweating

profusely by the top of the first hill. We stopped to drink from our water bottles.

Vanessa reminded me of my promise. "So, what does your Chinese horoscope say?"

"Well, I don't know the time I was born and I take it on faith that my birthday is the actual day."

"You mean it might not be your real birthday?"

"Yeah, weird huh? Anyway, if it is true then I'm a brown dog in the year of the white sheep. My lucky element is water and a good job for me would be a detective."

"No way!"

"Way. Of course I could also be a fisherman or a diplomat. I'm somewhat sceptical about it, just like I don't really believe the horoscopes in the paper." I put my water bottle back in its rack. "Do you want to pick up anything at the store?" I asked.

"Some munchies for our room would be a good idea."

We whipped down the hill and with screeching brakes pulled into the Tru Value Foods parking lot. Once we had each purchased several bags of chips and some chocolate bars we were ready to head off again.

"The Agricultural Hall is just around the corner," I said. We were performing my play at the Hall on Saturday night. "Let's check it out."

Hand-painted in big letters on the yellow siding over the front porch, it said: Mayne Island Agricultural Hall. There was a single wooden door for entering the Hall. A notice board and picnic table were on the right of the entrance. The windows were only along the sides of the building, and the yard was fenced in. A Private Property, No Trespassing sign was nailed to the fence.

"Excellent!" said Vanessa pointing. "Our poster for the play is already on the Hall's notice board."

I wanted to see the stage so we could figure out where to put the props. I tried the front door, but it was locked. "I'd really like to get a look inside," I said. "Keep watch while I hop the fence."

"Are you sure? The sign says no trespassing."

"I only want to see what the hall looks like. I don't think anyone would mind."

Vanessa went out to the road and looked in both directions. She nodded her head and gave me two thumbs up. The fence wasn't very high. I was over it in a flash. I quickly covered the fifteen feet to the closest window and cupped my hands to look through the dirt-streaked glass.

"Darn," I muttered.

"The shade is pulled down," I called over to Vanessa. I moved over to the next window.

Once again the shade was drawn, but this time I could hear muffled voices from inside the hall.

The person talking was female. "Don't think I'm not aware of what you're up to."

A male voice responded, "Jeannie, you've mistaken me for someone who cares. My activities are completely innocent and I dare you to prove otherwise."

"Oh, I will, I will. That's my job, remember?"

I had been standing on my tiptoes to hear them better. Unfortunately, I was still favouring my weak left leg. Suddenly my right calf cramped up and I fell against the wall for support.

"Did you hear something?" asked the male voice. Footsteps squeaked across the floor towards the window. I ducked down and tried to melt into the siding. The blinds were raised and then there was a moment of silence.

"Anything?"

"There's a kid out by the road, but that's all I can see."

"We're done. Just remember I'll be watching you."

"Go ahead . . . "

Footsteps moved away from the window to the front of the hall. Our bikes! I flew across the side yard, scrambled over the fence and hissed at Vanessa, "Grab your bike, now!"

We both sped off up the hill. I stole a glance back to see a smartly dressed woman cross the street to a green car. That must be Jeannie. A youngish man with long scraggly hair was standing in the doorway looking up at us.

"Keep pumping those legs," I urged.

"What happened?" Vanessa asked.

"I'll explain once we're out of sight."

We stopped to catch our breath around the first bend. I told Vanessa everything I had heard.

"Do mysteries follow you around or something? Here I thought we were taking a nice little vacation to relax and enjoy our final days of summer."

"It's probably nothing."

"Hah! Nothing with you means smugglers or gangsters or some other kind of trouble."

"No, honestly, I'm sure we can forget all about it. Come on, I'll race you."

It didn't take us long to get up the next hill and we were soon coasting towards the Davis ranch.

"That was easy!" Vanessa whooped as we reached the turn for their gravel driveway.

Mr. and Mrs. Davis had a beautiful two-story log house surrounded by spruce trees. To the right of the house was a white barn and next to that were the stables. A fenced off paddock was attached to the front of the stables. Two chestnut horses were standing lazily in the shade, their tails swishing at the clouds of buzzing flies.

"Hello!" I called out. "Anybody here?"

A husky woman's voice reverberated from the barn. "Be with you in a minute!"

There was a loud crash, some muffled cursing and then a tall middle-aged woman came striding out of the barn's side door.

"Darn rats! They're into the feed again. And that cat is useless." She turned to face the barn. "Rusty, you're not getting dinner until you catch that rat, do you hear me?"

Mrs. Davis shook her fist at the barn. Vanessa and I were both trying very hard not to laugh.

"Oh, go ahead and laugh. At least somebody should be enjoying this." She stuck out a weathered hand. "Autumn, great to see you again. And you must be Vanessa. Grab your gear and I'll show you to your room. Mr. Davis and the new hands should be back in a few minutes for lunch."

"Can we help you get lunch ready?" I asked.

"I never say no to someone lending me a hand. Just leave your bikes on the porch. We'll find a better place for them later."

Vanessa had obviously never been in a custom log home before. I could see she was impressed. "Wait until you see the rest of it," I said.

There were solid cedar timbers holding up the ceilings throughout the house.

"Look at how big the rooms are!" Vanessa commented. "So open and spacious."

"This style is called post and beam," said Mrs. Davis. "Even better, with a solid cedar log home the wood acts as its own insulation. When it's cold and windy outside, you still get this wonderfully warm, cozy feeling inside. I just love it."

We climbed the open staircase to the second floor and Mrs.

Davis pointed at the first door on our left.

"This will be your room for the next two weeks. I'll let you fight over the beds. The bathroom is at the end of the hallway. You can join me in the kitchen once you've unpacked."

"Would you mind if I had the bed by the window?" I asked Vanessa.

"Go for it. I'd prefer the wall anyway. I don't sleep very well if there's fresh air blowing on my face."

"Your horoscope said you should have an east side window open and the wind would be good for you."

Vanessa laughed. "I guess it was wrong!"

We put our clothes away, then I started to set out my small collection of self-defence gear.

Vanessa apparently couldn't resist. "Expecting a battle?"

"Mrs. Lee taught me how to use all of these. She said I had to practise regularly if I wanted to learn any more from her." I picked up a six-inch long piece of wood with rounded ends. "This one is my favourite. It's called a *yawara*."

"It's just a little stick! How could that be used for self-defence?"

"Remember the pressure points Mrs. Lee showed us?"

"Sure." Vanessa rubbed her elbow. "How could I forget?"

"Hit one of those points with the end of the yawara stick and it's like somebody dropped a ton of bricks on you."

"I'm glad Mrs. Lee is on our side. Will you demonstrate it for me?"

"Even better, you can be my training partner."

Vanessa's stomach suddenly growled. "Lunch and then horses. The self-defence training can come later. Much later, actually, if you're going to use me as a human pin cushion!"

We bounded down the stairs two at a time.

秋玉

7

Mrs. Davis was waiting for us in the kitchen. She obviously had a no nonsense approach to her work.

"Vanessa, you've got bread duty. Grab a knife and start slicing. Autumn, you can set the table and put out the condiments."

"How many slices should I cut?" asked Vanessa.

"It's not slices. It's loaves around here! Bruce and Jamie can eat three to four sandwiches each. You should start with that loaf and then about half of the other one."

Mr. Davis and the two ranch hands arrived just as everything was ready.

"Right on time," grinned Mr. Davis through the back door.

"I think not, Henry," scoffed Mrs. Davis. "I want to see freshly scrubbed faces and clean hands before the three of you are allowed to eat at my table."

"Oh, all right," Mr. Davis grumbled good-naturedly. "Come on, boys. I'm too hungry to argue."

Running water and loud splashing quickly ensued. The three men came back into the kitchen. Mrs. Davis gave her husband a friendly hug and began the introductions.

"Vanessa, Autumn, you've both met this incorrigible man I call a husband. These other two are Bruce and Jamie, our hired hands for the summer."

Neither of them looked happy to see us.

"Howdy," mumbled Jamie.

"Let's eat!" said Bruce.

The Davises sat at either end of the table. Vanessa and I were across from Jamie and Bruce. Vanessa was trying not to blush when Jamie looked at her. Jamie's long blonde hair was neatly tied back in a ponytail. His rugged facial features were in strong contrast to Bruce's black-rimmed glasses and short, neat brown hair.

"Autumn, would you like to say grace?" asked Mrs. Davis.

"Sure! We have our own way of doing it at home." I reached for Vanessa and Mr. Davis' hands. "Everyone hold hands and form a circle." I waited until Bruce and Jamie put down their utensils and the circle was complete. "Bless this food, bless this meal, thanks for all of us being together: Mr. Davis, Bruce, Jamie, Mrs. Davis, Vanessa, and Autumn. Amen."

"Thank you, Autumn," said Mrs. Davis. "That was very nicely done. Let the feeding frenzy begin."

She wasn't far off. I was beginning to wonder how they could afford to keep Bruce and Jamie around, the way they were eating.

"So," began Mr. Davis, "what do you two want to accomplish while you're here?"

"Well," I replied, "other than putting on the play I told you about, we just want to help out with the horses."

Mr. Davis winked at Jamie. "Well, I think we can keep you very busy then."

"I didn't see Dream Catcher when we came in." I said. "Is he out in the field today?"

Mr. Davis' face clouded over.

"Let me answer that," said Mrs. Davis. "Dream Catcher was never the same after you rescued him. He refused to race and we slowly went into debt. We had to sell him about a month ago."

Mr. Davis brightened again. "The good news is that Dream Catcher impregnated one of our gals before we sold him. We've got a mare that'll be giving birth to twins any day now. I bet you those little foals will be as fast as all get out! If you two could get things ready in the stable that would be a great start. We'll also start you with the horse grooming this afternoon — that way the horses will get to know you. Sound good?"

"Good?!" exclaimed Vanessa, then she blushed beet red. "I mean, that would be wonderful."

"Why would you want to do a play here?" scoffed Bruce.

"Mind your manners," Mrs. Davis reprimanded him. "I would love to hear about your play, Autumn."

"It's a story about a sing-song girl in 1930s Shanghai. The sing-song girls were usually bought at a young age. They spent most of their lives paying off their servitude by performing in the music halls of Shanghai. Sorrow, that's her name, discovers an abandoned baby. She gets a friend to help her play a trick on her owner in order to buy her freedom."

"You wrote it by yourself?" asked Mr. Davis.

"I do a lot of reading about old Shanghai. The idea for the play just popped into my head one night."

"That's quite amazing," said Mr. Davis. "I don't think I've ever had an idea pop into my head."

"I'd second that," Mrs. Davis agreed, winking at her husband. "Will you girls need a ride into the village? I can't imagine you riding your bikes back and forth late at night. The roads are too narrow for it to be safe after dark."

"If you don't mind," I said, "we would really appreciate a ride tomorrow after dinner. We're meeting a Mr. Terces at the Agricultural Hall."

"Mr. Terces?" Mrs. Davis stopped with a fork halfway to her mouth.

"Ahem," Mr. Davis cleared his throat.

"Oh, right, he's that director that's filming on the island. You bet I'll be driving you to your first meeting."

In less than twenty minutes the table was devoid of food. Mr. Davis pushed back his chair and excused himself.

"I'll be in the stable," said Jamie.

I started to collect the empty plates on the table.

Mrs. Davis shooed us away. "I'll clean up. I'm sure you're dying to meet the horses. Jamie will acquaint you girls with our four-legged family members."

The horse stable was a one-story wooden building to the right of the barn. The white paint was starting to peel in several places. There was a small, framed plaque next to the stable door. It read:

1. A man should in no way put himself in a situation where he will get injured.

2. The horse shall in no way be injured through man's anger, or any other way.

3. The horse must be put in a position where he feels good and rewarded after the training.

— Xenophon, father of classical equitation

"Who would name their kid Xenophon?" I snickered.

Vanessa lightly tapped my head. "Don't you know anything? He was this old Greek guy who wrote one of the first books on horses."

Jamie was already waiting for us inside.

"Ever groomed a horse before?" asked Jamie.

"I helped my cousin once," replied Vanessa.

"And I watched last year when I was visiting the Davises."

"Rookies," Jamie rolled his eyes. "It's not too difficult to pick up the basics, but your muscles are going to be pretty tired by dinner time. Don't think that'll get you off of doing your share of the chores, though. Just take it slow and easy today. It's more important that the horses get used to having you around, anyway."

There were six stalls on each side and one big stall at the back. Jamie pointed towards it.

"That's the birthing stall. We need to get it ready for Star, she'll be having her foals before the week is over."

Jamie introduced the horses. "The bay on your left is Sparkle. The young colt with her is Electric Blue."

"Oh, he's sooo cute!" Vanessa gushed.

"Next on this side we have Scamp, Periwinkle, Rainbow, and Saltine."

As Jamie said their names, the horses poked their heads out over the stall doors to see what was going on. Vanessa started to giggle. "I didn't know we were so interesting."

"Imagine how boring it is to just stand in your stall for hours! Of course we're worth a look-see. Most of these horses are owned by other people who only come out to ride them on the weekend."

"Oh," Vanessa sounded disappointed, "does that mean we can't ride them?"

"Part of our contract is to give them exercise. That's the best part of the job!" Jamie finished up his introductions, "Over here are Bart, Fly, Clip-Clop, Class Act, and finally, on your right is Star." The pregnant thoroughbred leisurely turned to inspect us.

"I think I just saw one of the foals kicking!" cried Vanessa.

"When you brush her, you'll be able to feel them for yourself. Okay, time to get to work."

Jamie walked over to a big closet and began pulling out equipment. "Autumn, take this lead and connect it to Sparkle's harness. Let her know what you're going to do as you open the stall door and walk her over to the grooming posts, outside and to your left."

I was feeling very nervous. I guess it showed.

"Relax," chided Jamie. "Keep your actions slow and fluid; horses don't like abrupt movements."

"Anything else?"

"When you walk around the horse, make sure you put your hand on her body so she knows where you are. If you walk behind her, you want to put your hand over her tail. That way she knows you're back there and doesn't accidentally kick you."

"Why would she want to kick me?"

"She might think you're a predator or an animal that wants to hurt her. Horses still rely on their instincts for survival."

"My uncle also said to talk to them all the time to help them know where you are," added Vanessa.

I pointed at the colt. "What about Electric Blue?"

"Don't worry. The little fellow will trot along after her. Vanessa, grab the bucket with the brushes and curry combs, I'll take the rest."

Jamie showed us how to hook Sparkle up to the grooming post. He then gave us a quick lesson. "We brush the horses every day. Start at the top of her neck and work your way to her rear." He picked up an oval shaped brush with soft rubber teeth. "Use the curry comb in a circular motion to get all of the loose hair and scurf, that's horse dirt, out of the horse's coat."

Vanessa pulled another curry comb out of the bucket and

started on the other side.

"Once you're done, take the dandy brush and use long strokes with its stiff bristles to brush all of the loose stuff off."

Jamie handed me the dandy brush and I gave it a try. "Autumn, try the same motion you would use when sweeping a floor. You flick the brush away and up from the coat so that all the dirt comes off."

Jamie pulled a third brush out of the bucket. "The body brush is meant to smooth down the hair and to get rid of any traces of leftover dirt after you have thoroughly used the dandy brush. With the body brush, don't use a flicking motion. Instead, you smooth it flat over the horse's coat to flatten the hair. This brush often gives the horse a shiny, clean appearance. They love it. It's like a massage!"

I could feel Sparkle relaxing as I ran the body brush along her side.

"One final thing," Jamie held up a strange hook-shaped tool.

"I know what that is," said Vanessa. "It's a hoof pick!"

"Do you know how to use it?" asked Jamie

"I think so. You have to pick up the horse's foot." Vanessa ran her hand down Sparkle's leg then gently squeezed her ankle. "Autumn, make sure not to pick up the horse's foot too high, or she might lose her balance. When you use the hoof pick, always scrape away from you, just as you would if you were using a carrot peeler."

"Very good, Vanessa. I'll finish her off with a towel. Vanessa, you can start on Electric Blue and Autumn, I'll bring you Scamp."

Jamie left us to work on our own. Once we had groomed the horses, Bruce wandered by. "I'll meet you two at the horse paddock in ten minutes."

Bruce was a bit more reserved, and certainly not as smooth a talker as Jamie. He knew a lot about training horses, though. We were almost finished when Jamie showed up at the entrance to the paddock. He was urgently beckoning to Bruce.

"What now?" Bruce cursed under his breath. "Excuse me," he apologized.

Jamie's eyes kept looking our way as he delivered his message. Bruce was slowly nodding his head like he wasn't in total agreement. Eventually he seemed to give in. That's when he came back over to us.

"I've got an errand to run with Jamie. Fifteen more minutes with Bart here and then do the same with Fly. If I'm not back, you know where everything should be put away. Oh, and muck out the stalls as well."

Once they were gone Vanessa stopped working and stared at me.

"What?"

"I'm trying to see if I can spot the aura around you."

"Why?"

"I saw this movie once about two girls who went to help out on a horse ranch. Not once did anybody have a mysterious conversation or act all weird. You definitely have a special gift for attracting strange goings-on."

"Maybe we're just reading too much into this," I replied.

"Right, could be Jamie wanted help with his . . . " she hesitated.

"His ponytail?" I dead-panned.

Vanessa blushed. Then we both cracked up.

秋玉

8

I had a nice long shower before dinner. Feeling refreshed and several pounds lighter without all the dirt, I headed down for dinner.

Vanessa was visibly disappointed that Jamie wasn't at the table.

"You'll have to excuse the boys," said Mr. Davis. "They had some work to do in the . . . " he hesitated, " . . . in the upper field."

Mrs. Davis glared at her husband. "Couldn't someone, like you my dear husband, have mentioned that to me earlier? Maybe before I made all this food, hmmm?"

Dinner was a very quiet affair. Mr. and Mrs. Davis appeared to be arguing with just their eyes, and neither Vanessa nor I had the energy to carry on an intelligent conversation. By the time we were ready for bed, Jamie and Bruce had still not returned. The tension in the house was palpable.

"Was that ever painful!" commented Vanessa once we were in our room.

I thought about trying out the wireless connection to the Internet to check my email, but I wasn't up to the challenge of wrestling with new technology. Vanessa hadn't mentioned doing any martial arts training either. I pulled out a small notebook from under my pillow.

"What's that you're writing in? It's not the notebook you usually have with you."

"I call it my 'Dear Ghost Mother Diary'."

Vanessa looked puzzled. "Your what?"

"Ghost Mother Diary. I use it because my birth mother in China is like a ghost to me. Mary Blue, the social worker I saw last month, suggested I write down my feelings and thoughts even though I'll probably never meet my birth parents. Mrs. Lee came up with the name."

"That's really sad. Do you think your birth mother is still alive?"

"No reason she wouldn't be — my birth father, too. What's even weirder to think about is that I probably have younger and older siblings in China as well."

"No way!"

"I can't say for sure, but some of the research my parents have collected makes it look like I might have a whole ghost family somewhere over in China."

"What do you write in there? Could you read me part of the diary?"

"I guess so, if you promise not to laugh or tell anyone else."

"Cross my heart."

"Okay," I thumbed through to my earliest entry.

"Dear Ghost Mother, People often say to my parents: 'how lucky she is — her life is so much better here.' I always like what my mom says in response: 'Every child is entitled to have a family.' But then I read about how fast China is changing. I know I've got it good here: my parents are wonderful and I have really great friends . . . "

Vanessa mimed, "Moi?"

" . . . like Adam and Vanessa and Mrs. Lee. But still, would my life have been so different in China if we had stayed together as a family? And of course, the answer to that is always that life is like a game of cards (where did Mary Blue learn this stuff anyway) and you gotta go with the hand you're dealt. Speculating whether or not my life would have been better, worse or just the same is pointless. So, ghost mother of mine, I sometimes wonder about you and my ghost father and maybe even about ghost brothers and sisters. Often I'm sorry you are only a ghost. Take care, your white tiger."

"Wow! Thanks for sharing that with me, Autumn. I'm not sure how I'd be handling such big feelings."

"You just make it up as you go, I guess."

"Why did you sign it 'your white tiger'?"

"Long ago, Chinese people believed that four mythical animals ruled the cardinal directions: the West was ruled by a white tiger, the North by a black tortoise, the South by a red phoenix, and the East by a green dragon. I live in the West and when I was a kid, I always wanted to be a tiger. It seemed somehow appropriate to sign it that way."

Vanessa yawned. "Oops, sorry. Look at the time! I'm too exhausted to imagine doing this all over again tomorrow. Lights out?"

"Yep, have a good sleep."

"Night."

My eyes opened wide. I was vaguely aware of an unusual sound that had brought me out of a deep sleep.

"Kweighhh . . . " There it was again. Vanessa was nestled under her covers. I parted the curtains and tried to find where the strange sound was coming from.

"Kweighhh . . . " The moon was just coming up. Silhouetted on the hill behind the barn was something that sort of looked like a goat, but no goat I'd ever seen. There was a long horn coming straight off of its forehead and it had a shaggy tail like an ox. It looked exactly like the Chinese unicorn in my dream. UNICORN? No way . . .

I gave Vanessa's body a nudge. "Vanessa, wake up, you have to see this!"

"Huh, what time is it?"

"Kweighhh . . . "

"That's a funny noise," she yawned.

"I've been trying to tell you. Come take a look. I think there's a unicorn on the hill outside."

Vanessa flopped out of bed and staggered to the window. "Where?"

I started to point but the creature was gone.

Vanessa sighed. "Right. I'm going back to sleep. Please don't get me up again unless it's standing in our room."

I lay awake for a long time wondering about what I had just seen.

* * *

"We need to learn more about Chinese unicorns," suggested Amy.

"I doubt if my Uncle knows anything about them," said Soo-Lin. "Could we ask Sergei?"

"Didn't you hear?" said Qiu Yu. "After his restaurant was destroyed, he decided to take Lucky and travel to America. Amy received a postcard from him about a month ago. He's in New York now. He hoped we were all well and wanted to tell us that life is wonderful over there. He's started a restaurant with some old friends and they're very busy."

"Qiu Yu, what about your Aunt? I know you can't stand her, but she might be able to help us."

"Actually, things seem to be changing for the better with my Aunt. I think I finally understand her. I had no idea that Auntie's bound feet caused her such excruciating pain all the time. She's hidden it pretty well from me, until recently."

"It's a barbaric custom and so disgusting," exclaimed Amy. "I'm glad it was finally outlawed."

Soo-Lin clenched and unclenched her fists. "Amy, don't go talking like that when you don't know a thing about it. Golden Lilies, as my mother called them, greatly enhanced a young girl's opportunity for making a good marriage. It was an expected part of Chinese society, unless you were a peasant or poor like my family. Okay?"

Amy stuck out her hand. "Oh, Soo-Lin, please accept my sincerest apology. I didn't mean to upset you. Friends?"

Soo-Lin looked at the outstretched hand and calmed down. She grabbed Amy and gave her fierce hug. "Of course we're friends. I'm twice indebted to you. You rescued my brother from the wheels of a rickshaw and you helped save my Uncle's life. I'm afraid you're stuck with me forever."

The girls had arrived at Qiu Yu's house. The gate opened to a small courtyard between the outer wall and the one-story compound.

"Auntie!" cried out Qiu Yu. "I'm home."

One of the servants poked a head out of the kitchen window. "Auntie in here. Come, come." He seemed excited and happy, as he waved them through the doorway.

Qiu Yu couldn't believe her eyes. Her aunt was sitting at the kitchen table, sharing a plate of fresh pastries with the servants. This certainly wasn't the same Auntie Shu-Shu. She was calmer and more cheerful than Qiu Yu had ever seen her.

"Qiu Yu, manners please."

"Right! Auntie, I'd like to introduce my friends, Soo-Lin and Amy. Amy, Soo-Lin, this is my Auntie Shu-Shu."

"Welcome, girls. Please join me for tea."

Amy and Soo-Lin hesitated but decided it was best to sit down. This certainly didn't look like the dragon lady Qiu Yu kept telling them about.

Qiu Yu decided on the direct approach. "Auntie, are you on drugs?"

"No," she grinned.

"Did you fall on your head?"

"No," she laughed.

"What then? I've never seen you so happy."

"I went to see an old acupuncturist in the walled city this morning. He stuck needles in my body and suddenly the pain stopped."

She held out one of her tiny, silk-slippered feet. "If I could dance on these useless things, I would be doing it right now."

"Ahem," Amy cleared her throat and raised her eyebrows.

Qiu Yu shook her head. Chinese decorum required idle chitchat before they could get down to business. She used the excuse of passing a plate of sweets to glare sternly at her friend. After another ten minutes of pleasantries, she broached the subject.

"Auntie, we were wondering what you could tell us about *zhi*, Chinese unicorns? We have a friend who thinks she's met one."

Auntie Shu-Shu took a moment to collect her thoughts. "The zhi has always been treasured by women, and by others who suffer under the burden of great injustice. In fact, all Chinese people seem to have an innate understanding of the true meaning and significance of the zhi, for it always reappears in times of war or other social upheaval — when the need for justice and mercy is at its greatest. It has a wonderful capacity for perpetual resurrection in different places and at different times. With the Japanese army committing terrible acts of injustice daily throughout our country, I'm not surprised to find people once again longing for the incorruptible power of the mythic zhi."

"So it could be real?" asked Amy.

"You find it and then you can tell me!" laughed Auntie. She changed the subject by suggesting the girls stay for lunch.

After a delightful meal, the girls thanked Auntie Shu-Shu for her kind hospitality.

"Come again, any time. Qiu Yu, I'd like to speak to you privately for a minute."

Qiu Yu asked the others to wait for her in the courtyard.

Auntie Shu-Shu began rummaging through a black lacquered box covered with finely detailed red peony petals.

"Ah, here they are." She handed three small ceramic vials to her niece. "Take these, just in case."

"In case of what, Auntie?"

"If there really is a zhi you need to fill these vials. A tear in one, blood in the second and hair from its mane in the third."

"Why?"

"Legend has it that the person who keeps these parts of a zhi will be wealthy and powerful beyond their wildest dreams. Be prepared! Remember though, that you will never be able to share what you have collected with anyone but a true believer. Don't miss out on the opportunity if it comes to you. Listen to your Auntie. Understand?"

"Yes, I will. Thank you, Auntie." Qiu Yu stuffed the ceramic vials into an inner pocket of her padded jacket. She left to catch up with her friends. Wealth and power, she liked the sound of that!

秋玉

9

Jamie and Bruce already had their plates piled high with toast, ham and farm fresh eggs.

"Hey, guys! Leave some for us," Vanessa complained. Getting up with the roosters hadn't put Vanessa in a very good mood.

Jamie looked up and I was shocked to see an obvious black eye. That's also when I noticed that Bruce was eating with his left hand today. His right arm was held close to his chest like his ribs were hurting him.

Their condition hadn't escaped the watchful eye of Mrs. Davis either. "Nice shiner, Jamie. You boys weren't fighting last night, were you?"

"No, Mrs. Davis. I found a tree that had fallen onto a section of fencing. We were cutting it up when it kicked back on us. Bruce took it on the chest and then he fell onto me."

"Let me see those ribs," she demanded.

Bruce briefly lifted up his shirt for Mrs. Davis. I caught myself before gasping out loud. The mark at the centre of the bruise over his ribs resembled a hoof print! Vanessa kicked me under the table. She must have seen it, too.

Mrs. Davis harrumphed loudly. "You need to see a doctor. It's still early enough to catch the ferry over to Saltspring Island. I'll call the clinic and let them know you're coming."

Bruce looked at Jamie, then at Mrs. Davis. "I don't think I can drive . . . " His eyes rolled back into their sockets and he fainted.

Mrs. Davis caught his forehead before it could slam into the table. "Jamie, go get Mr. Davis from the barn. You girls keep him from falling while I call the doctor's office."

Vanessa and I moved to the other side of the table. Jamie dashed out the door and Mrs. Davis went hunting for the phone number.

"Did you see his bruise?" whispered Vanessa.

I nodded my head. "Hoof print," I coughed.

Vanessa motioned to lift up his shirt for another look. I was reaching for it when Bruce moaned and slowly came to. I quickly pulled back my arm and pretended to fix my hair.

Mr. Davis and Jamie arrived and we all helped move Bruce gently out to Jamie's truck. "I'll take him," Jamie volunteered before anyone else could offer.

"You girls up to taking on some extra chores today?" asked Mr. Davis.

We both reluctantly nodded. It was going to be a long day.

"Okay, lad, go. And have them check out your eye while you're there."

Mr. Davis shook Jamie's hand. I thought I saw a piece of folded paper being exchanged from one palm to the other. A note? Vanessa was going to love this!

"You girls go finish your breakfast. You'll need the extra energy today," Mr. Davis chuckled.

"Yes, sir," I agreed.

Mr. Davis followed us back into the kitchen. Darn. I'd have to wait until we were alone to tell Vanessa about the note.

We chatted amiably with the Davises over breakfast. The tension from last night had disappeared the moment Bruce and Jamie left. Vanessa and I helped Mrs. Davis clean up and then we excused ourselves to brush our teeth.

By the top of the stairs I was ready to explode. "I thought we'd never be alone."

"Why?"

"I'd swear I saw a note being passed from Mr. Davis to Jamie. I would give anything to know what it said."

Vanessa paused on the landing. "I don't think Bruce and Jamie will be coming back."

"Hmmm," I said, zipping my lips. "The bathroom," I mouthed.

I closed the bathroom door and turned on the water so we couldn't be overheard. "I bet you're right. I saw something last night that I think was more than a goat and Bruce has a hoof print on his chest. It wasn't just a dream."

"Do you think the whole scene this morning was staged for our benefit?"

"No! Well, maybe. Bruce did appear to be in real pain."

"Oh," Vanessa covered her mouth, "could he have faked the fainting and heard us talking?"

"I hope not. Let's stay alert and watch for anything else suspicious."

Mr. Davis had a list with him. "I've written out everything that needs to get done today. You can start by feeding the horses and then let them out into the field for some exercise. The stalls need mucking out and today is bath day for all of the horses. Call me when you've reached that point and I'll help you out."

I had never worked so hard in my life. My left leg began acting up and the day became one big blur. I couldn't even remember if we'd stopped for lunch. By the time we had cleaned up for dinner we were both too tired to care about anything mysterious.

"Jamie called," said Mrs. Davis. "They'll be staying overnight."

Vanessa groaned.

"We need Adam," I suggested. "May I use the phone?"

"Sure, Autumn, go right ahead."

I dialled the number for Adam's house but it went straight to the answering machine. I left a brief message and told Adam we would email him with more details.

"Mr. Davis, when Adam comes can he bring my dog Watson with him?"

Mr. Davis looked worried. "I don't know . . . "

Mrs. Davis cut him off. "Of course he can bring Watson! He was such a cute puppy. I was surprised you didn't have him with you."

"Well. Mr. Davis was worried about the horses . . . "

"Worried? That dog was born on a farm, he knows all about horses." She glared at Mr. Davis. "Henry, I thought you told me that Autumn didn't want to bring her dog? I'd love to see if Watson remembers the tricks I taught him as a pup. I won't hear another word about it. I'll even train him to work with the horses if you'd like."

"Thanks!"

Mrs. Davis looked at her watch. "Say, Autumn, aren't you girls going to the Agricultural Hall tonight to meet that man about your play?"

"I'm so tired I'd completely forgotten about it. I'll send Adam an email and then we'll be ready."

Vanessa and I went up to our room. I was close to the window as I was gathering up my things.

"I'm such an idiot!" I exclaimed.

"What?"

"Look out the window. Do you see anything strange?"

Vanessa parted the curtains and peered outside. "Where?"

"Down by the garage."

"No. There's nothing down there."

"Exactly."

"I have no idea what you're talking about."

"Think back. That little one-horse trailer that was stored behind the garage isn't there anymore. My brain registered it this morning, but I've been too tired to put the pieces together."

"Okay, but so what? None of the horses are missing."

I snapped my fingers. "The unicorn! I bet Jamie and Bruce took it with them."

"The unicorn, Autumn? You've got unicorns on the brain. I'm having a hard time believing in a unicorn when everything so far says it's only a goat or a small pony."

"I haven't told you this, but since I saw that strange animal on the hillside, I can sense that something is out there. There, I've said it. Don't laugh or I won't mention it again."

I turned on the handheld computer and launched the email program.

Subject: Get your butt over here!

Adam, hope you're ready to join us. The two new ranch hands, Jamie and Bruce, are gone and Vanessa and I are exhausted from working so hard. We could really use your big manly muscles (oops, Vanessa just blushed!) to help us out. BTW, Vanessa says I have an aura that attracts mysteries. So guess what? I'm sure I saw a Chinese unicorn last night! We need to go exploring and I want you here with us. Mrs. Davis says that Watson is welcome as well. Please bring him with you. I'm sure he'll be thrilled. Hugs and kisses (ha, ha, made her blush again),

Autumn

I pressed the send button just as Mrs. Davis called at us from downstairs. "You girls ready to go?"

"Coming," we replied.

秋玉

10

It was very kind of Mrs. Davis to drive us to the Agricultural Hall. She turned left at the end of the gravel driveway and headed towards Miners Bay Village.

"So, Autumn, tell me more about your play," said Mrs. Davis.

"Well, it's based on some stories I've written about three girls who live in Shanghai in the 1930s. In the play they help out a sing-song girl. Like I said before, it was a popular form of entertainment in old Shanghai. The girls would dress up in fancy silk outfits. They were carried around in sedan chairs to different music halls to sing for the clientele."

"Your play does sounds like it will be fun," said Mrs. Davis. "Do you think you'll be ready by Saturday?"

"It should only take a few rehearsals. Vanessa and I have already been practising the play together. Adam will be arriving later in the week to help out during the play. All we need is to see the actual stage and figure out our stage movements. We're hoping Mr. Terces can help us with that."

"Have you met him before?"

"Nope. I sent an email to the Mayne Island Chamber of

Commerce and he was the one who replied. We've sent notes back and forth about the play and he agreed to help us out. He's also the one who put up the posters for us. You're welcome to come meet him if you'd like." I sneaked a smile at Vanessa. Mrs. Davis was very nice, but she did appear to be woven of the same cloth as Mrs. Chandler!

Mrs. Davis put on her left turn signal and slowed down for the entrance to the Agricultural Hall's small parking lot. "I'll just make sure everything is okay," she stated.

As we climbed out of the car, the front door to the hall opened. A young man came sauntering down the stairs. He was the man I'd overheard in the Hall the day before, the same one who had watched us cycle up the hill! He'd tied back his scraggly hair with a rubber band.

"He looks like a nerd," Mrs. Davis whispered into my ear.

"Autumn Parker?" he asked in a soft voice.

I stuck out my hand. "That's me!" I replied.

He certainly had a limp handshake. "Welcome! I'm Xavier Terces. Let's head inside. I'm very excited about your play."

Guess he didn't recognize us. Good.

I turned to Mrs. Davis and mouthed, "Well?"

"He seems harmless enough," she whispered. Then louder she said, "Call me once you're done, or sooner if you'd like to come home, okay?"

"Sure, thanks!"

Mr. Terces held the door open and waved us through. "Straight ahead is the main hall. The stage is very small and there's only seating for sixty people, but I think it will be fine for performing your play."

The stage was indeed tiny, but the hall had a warm, comfortable feeling. "I like it!" I declared.

Vanessa and I jumped up on the stage and mimed part of the first scene.

"So what do you need in the way of props and scenery?" asked Mr. Terces.

"Not too much . . . a round table, two wooden chairs, and a tea set."

I paced out the back of the stage with my feet. "Hmmm, about twelve feet. We should be fine. I can't think of anything else. Vanessa?"

"Maybe a tape deck to play music during the scene changes?" she suggested.

"No problem," said Mr. Terces. "I should be able to find everything you need by your next rehearsal."

There was a loud creak from behind the stage and the smartly dressed woman with the green car stepped out. Mr. Terces didn't look happy to see her.

"Excuse me," he apologized. "I'll be right back." He followed her behind the stage curtains as Vanessa and I stared at each other.

"She looks like Secret Service or FBI," I quietly commented.

"Yeah, right," Vanessa teased. "I'm sure that bulge under her jacket is a holster."

"What would she want with Mr. Terces?" I wondered out loud.

"None of our business, Autumn! Let's check out the lighting while we're waiting for him."

The stage faced out at an empty hall. Overhead were six canister lights that had plates for adding coloured gel filters. There was a reasonably new curtain for the front of the stage and a faded black one covering the back wall and side entrances.

The back curtain was pushed aside and a worried looking Mr. Terces returned. "Sorry about that, just a reporter from the Saltspring News. Now where were we? Oh, yes, when did you want to do a full rehearsal of your play? I can get you the table and chairs by tomorrow evening if you'd like to meet here again. Say around seven?"

"I don't see why not," I agreed. "Do you have a phone number where we can reach you if there's a change of plans?"

Mr. Terces started to perspire. "Er, no," he stammered. "My phone is out of order. Sending email is the only way to reach me."

"Same address as before?"

"Ah, yeah, that should do."

Mr. Terces locked the hall behind him and we said our good-byes. I could see that Vanessa was ready to burst. Once we were out of earshot she blurted, "But don't you need a phone line to get your email?"

I had to think for a minute. "Well, not necessarily. He could have a wireless connection to the Internet. Dad said that Mayne Island has put in a wireless network that covers the entire island. That's why I can check my own email and send messages. But I agree that it's very suspicious that he wouldn't give us his phone number."

I pulled out my cell phone and called Mrs. Davis.

"Sorry, Autumn, I'm in the middle of baking some pies. Could you two visit Miners Bay for half an hour? I'll meet you there once I'm done."

Miners Bay was already pretty much shut down for the night. We slowly meandered down the hill to the village.

"Hey, isn't that Mr. Terces going into the Miners Bay Trading Post?" Vanessa pointed.

"Want to follow him?"

"Sure," Vanessa eagerly nodded in agreement.

The Trading Post was still open so we went inside. I quickly glanced around. But Mr. Terces was nowhere in sight!

The proprietor behind the counter was staring hard at me. "You look familiar, young lady. Don't I know you from somewhere? Wait, don't tell me, it'll come in a minute." He screwed up his face and pressed his fingertips to his temples. "It's coming . . . July . . . you had a young man with you . . . very polite fellow . . . you were looking for some friends . . . Chinese? Yes, Chinese. How am I doing so far?"

"Right on all counts!" I laughed. "That was very impressive. How do you remember so much, when we were only briefly in your store?"

"I'll teach you a little trick that my grade four teacher once taught our class. I make up ice cream sundaes to remember things. Don't take offence, but an Oreo, banana sundae with four Chinese nuts for a topping was all it took to recall your little visit."

Mrs. Lee had once called me a banana as well — yellow on the outside and white on the inside. I did not like the reference at all. I'm sure that nobody had called Adam an Oreo before, at least not to his face, and I know he wouldn't have liked it either.

Vanessa could see I was getting angry. She joined in with, "I've got one for you. What if three old ladies came into your store and bought a bag of chips, a box of tea and a newspaper?"

"What kind of chips and do they have any distinguishing features?" he countered.

Vanessa thought for a moment. "Salt and vinegar. My personal favourite, and one of the ladies has a wart in her forehead."

"That's easy, then," he chuckled. "Three scoops of liquorice ice cream, one covered in French fries, the second with a single walnut, and the third with a slice of processed cheese. A red rose would be added as a garnish."

"And you'd remember all that?" Vanessa said.

"Yes."

"And even if one of them walked into your store five years from now?" I challenged.

"Well, to be honest, the one with the wart on her head would be the kicker. If she had surgery to remove it or if the other two came in without her I might have some trouble getting it right."

Mrs. Davis came through the door. She must have heard this all before. "You two didn't fall for Bill's old ice cream sundae story, did you?"

"Now, now, Sally . . . "

"Girls, Mr. Dibble here has a photographic memory. That baloney he just fed you is pure horse manure."

Mr. Dibble had turned red. "Sorry, ladies. If I'd known you were staying with Sally, I . . . well . . . I'm sorry."

Vanessa giggled and I politely thanked him for entertaining us while we waited.

"Come on, girls," said Mrs. Davis, "you have a big day ahead of you tomorrow."

I suddenly realized that we had forgotten all about Mr. Terces. Had Mr. Dibble been distracting us from looking for him? What was going on here? Was everyone involved?

秋玉

11

The rain was dropping out of the sky in heavy waves. It smashed onto the rooftops, overflowed the gutters and was flooding the yard. The rainstorm must have started after we went to bed. Jamie knocked on our door, urging us to come right away. We quickly dressed and followed him outside.

We ran the thirty feet to the barn door and were completely soaked. Jamie led us to the birthing stall at the rear of the barn.

"I thought you were staying on Saltspring tonight," I ventured.

Jamie gave me a peculiar stare and changed the subject. "The first foal was stillborn. Mortality in foals is higher for twins than in single births. Mr. Davis is working to save the other foal."

In the dimly lit stall Mr. Davis had worked a tiny head halfway out of the birth canal. A small tarp-covered mound lay in the far corner. Vanessa poked me to make sure I'd seen it.

"Girls!" Mr. Davis called to them. "Quick, I need your help! Autumn, stroke Star's head. Vanessa, talk to her in a soothing voice. Jamie, it's going to take both of us to get this foal safely out."

The mare was lying on her right side in the birthing position. The tips of the foal's front hooves could just be seen emerging from the mother. Powerful contractions were pushing the foal from her body.

Mr. Davis stood up. "Whew, it's going okay now. We'll let the mother do the work." He stepped in after the umbilical cord had been broken in order to disinfect and tie it.

Star was looking very lovingly at the newborn foal.

The foal took a while to get up to her feet, and a while longer to get the hang of staying there. Eventually, she realized that in all the looking around, she had forgotten a very important fact: she was hungry! She tried to grab a nipple, and it must have tickled because Star jumped and the foal fell right down on her tender little nose.

Back to her feet, finally, then down again; up; down; up; down, until finally she got to her Mom's side and reached for the nipple. Star moved again. The foal was not amused. She stamped her little foot and glared at her mom. She let out a little neigh and went for the nipple again. This time she made it!

She grabbed the nipple and stood there for a minute, looking around as though saying "Uh, now what?" Finally she got the idea and started sucking with gusto. She wasted no time once she'd figured it out.

"The next few feedings contain colostrum, the mother's first milk, rich in protein and protective antibodies," said Mr. Davis. "It'll help her get a good start on life."

Jamie made sure the placenta had been completely delivered by Star. Then they both watched for the foal to pass her first manure so they would know that her digestive system was working properly.

Star was a wonderful and very trusting mother. She had no problem with us annoying her baby. The foal, on the other hand, very quickly got tired of us and demanded in no uncertain terms that we leave her alone with her mother. After all, being born was hard work!

While Mr. Davis and Jamie were giving the foal her first shot, I noticed Vanessa wander over and peek under the tarp. She was pretending to tie her shoe. The look of surprise and shock on Vanessa's face was hard for her to hide.

I yawned loudly. "I think we better get back to bed!"

"Night, girls and thanks," said Mr. Davis. "Enjoy what's left of your sleep."

As we crossed the front yard Vanessa said, "I wish you could have seen it, I don't think it was dead! That foal was more like a goat, with the stub of a single horn on its forehead. It wasn't like any horse I've ever seen."

"You mean it was more like my Chinese unicorn? Now do you believe me?"

"Yes, Autumn, now I do. Whatever's going on around here, it's not just your imagination."

We had almost reached the house when I thought I spotted someone in black rain gear crossing the paddock towards the barn.

"Vanessa, hold up."

"I saw him, too."

"Let's go in the house, but sneak out again using the kitchen door."

We removed our boots, shook off as much rain as possible and quickly tiptoed through the house. I had my hand on the doorknob and was about to turn it when Mr. Davis' face appeared in the glass.

Vanessa gasped behind me. I opened the door and tried to cover up. "I thought the door might be locked and came to open it for you."

"Thanks," he gruffly replied. "Time for bed, young ladies."

Back in our room I turned off the light and slowly parted the curtains. It took several seconds for our eyes to adjust.

"Now that doesn't look normal," Vanessa whispered.

Three men in dark coats were dragging the baby unicorn into the field behind the house.

"We have to follow them. Are you game?"

"How are we going to get out? Mr. Davis is probably downstairs guarding the doors."

I opened the window and peered through the rain. "That's how." I pointed at a rickety wooden ladder just sitting on the roof. "Mr. Davis must have left it there."

"I hope you're right."

I put on my boots and rain jacket. "I'll meet you down below."

The rain-soaked cedar shakes were very slippery. Twice I almost took the quick way down, but I made it to the ladder and eased it over the side of the roof. Vanessa steadied the top as I slowly backed my way down to the ground. In return, I held it for her.

We stayed in the shadows, silently following the three men. They were talking in hushed voices and we couldn't make out what they were saying. Judging by their builds, two of the men could have easily been Bruce and Jamie. If only we could get a better look at them!

"They're heading to Campbell Bay," I whispered.

"But why . . . "

I shrugged as we started scrambling down a narrow trail. Vanessa stopped suddenly and pointed with her mouth hanging open.

"What is it?"

"Look!"

The three men were in a small rubber raft, paddling into the middle of the bay. A black tower, as tall as a truck, was visible above the water.

"No . . . "

"Yes, it's a submarine. No boat looks like that."

"But what's a submarine doing here? They didn't look like they were from the Navy."

The men passed the wrapped body to the waiting crew. Then they boarded the sub and stowed the raft. Once they were inside, the submarine silently disappeared into the dark waters of Campbell Bay.

The rain was coming down heavier again. Thunder could be heard in the distance. It made going back up the trail very difficult.

"I wish Adam were here," sighed Vanessa.

"I'll send him another email when we get to our room."

"He's going to be very upset if he misses this adventure. I hope he stops ignoring your notes."

"I know he'll come through for us," I boasted. "He's never let me down before." But deep down, I wasn't really sure if he would.

秋玉

12

The three girls stood in the shadows, fifty feet from Sorrow's private entrance, waiting for her to appear.

"I read a great description in the paper about the Great World," whispered Amy. "It has six floors of things to do, and each floor is different. The entire building is studded with every variety of entertainment Chinese ingenuity could contrive."

"How are we going to get in?"

"I've brought disguises for all of us. Soo-Lin, you'll be a merchant with your mistress. That's you, Qiu Yu, at her side."

"What about you? Your red hair is a dead giveaway."

"No problem. One bowler hat, a little fake moustache, an American accent and voila, I'm Randy the Reporter."

"How many times have you done this before?" asked Qiu Yu.

"Lots, but please don't tell my father. He worries too much about me all alone on the streets of Shanghai."

Soo-Lin and Qiu Yu both giggled uncontrollably as they put on their own disguises.

The ornate gate door swung inwards. Two men dressed in maroon silk robes carried out Sorrow's one-passenger sedan chair.

They held onto long horizontal poles that extended along both sides of the chair.

Once they were on their way, the three girls slowly pedalled their bicycles at a discreet distance. The two bearers were quite nimble at manoeuvring through the streets. In no time they had reached the performer's entrance of the Great World entertainment centre.

"She's sooo . . . beautiful," gasped Soo-Lin as Sorrow stepped onto the street.

A thick layer of white paint covered Sorrow's face. Her costume consisted of loose satin trousers in a pale yellow hue, with a broad black satin hem and a bright blue satin coat fastened upon the shoulder and reaching almost to her knees with a slit in either side-seam.

On her head Sorrow wore a coif of black satin embroidered with pearls, open at the top but coming low over the forehead and covering the ears, while artificial flowers and gold hairpins adorned the knot of shiny black hair at the back. Her feet were encased in red and gold silk slippers.

Sorrow waved with her hand towards the front entrance. The girls took their cue and moved around to the front of the massive building.

"Ready?" asked Amy. "I'll go first and meet you inside."

Amy went through the big entrance and Qiu Yu and Soo-Lin quickly followed. No one challenged them. A wall of noise and perspiring bodies greeted them as they stepped through the doors.

Along one long wall were gambling tables and slot machines. People of many countries were lined up six and seven deep around the tables.

Wandering around the floor were acrobats and musicians.

"Watch out for pickpockets," warned Soo-Lin. "I recognize some of the people in the crowd."

Sagging tables were piled high with goods for sale: fireworks, fans, stick incense, ginger, and birdcages with or without birds, in every imaginable form.

"How can those birds survive in here?" shouted Amy.

Sorrow had asked the girls to meet her near the centre of the floor. There was a small auditorium where for a few coins a person could watch the sing-song girls perform.

"There she is," pointed Qiu Yu.

Sorrow waved them off and nodded towards the stairs to the next floor. The three girls followed along, keeping a safe distance behind her. Amy and Qiu Yu kept in character with their disguises, but Soo-Lin couldn't stop giggling.

The din on the second floor was quite possibly louder than the first. Restaurants filled the floor, frying oil, steaming pots and edible creatures from all four animal kingdoms did a full assault on their senses. Actors in small groups entertained the seated restaurant patrons. Barbers and earwax extractors had their chairs and professional paraphernalia set up in every conceivable inch of free space.

Sorrow continued up to the third floor.

Soo-Lin leaned over to shout in Qiu Yu's ear. "I can't imagine what they have on the other four floors!"

The reduced noise level on the third floor was almost as much of a shock as the ear pounding sounds they'd just passed through. A variety of ice-cream parlours and herbal medicine shops lined the two sides of the floor. Near the middle were jugglers, photographers and a bevy of girls, their high-collared gowns slit to reveal their hips.

Sorrow beckoned to them and they joined her behind a fountain full of slowly melting ice sculptures.

"This place is exhausting," moaned Amy.

"I know what you mean," agreed Qiu Yu. "Can you imagine having to work here every day? Oops, sorry, Sorrow."

The fourth floor more than made up for the relative calm of the third. This time it was shooting galleries, fantan tables and massage benches filled with sweaty half-naked bodies. The girls looked the other way and followed Sorrow up a narrower staircase to the next level.

The three girls were wondering what new and bizarre entertainment would assault them and there it was, a stuffed whale hanging from the ceiling. Beneath its dust-covered body were girls with dresses slit to their armpits. Surrounding the girls were storytellers, a mirror maze, balloons, two love-letter booths with scribes who guaranteed results and even a temple filled with ferocious gods and burning joss sticks.

Finally they climbed the last set of stairs and reached the top floor of this amazing building. Tightrope walkers slithered back and forth overhead. For those who still had any money left, there were lottery ticket booths and marriage brokers.

The girls followed Sorrow to the far end of the floor. An area was closed off with rainbow coloured curtains.

Sorrow looked very disappointed. "The unicorn was in there before. But I don't see the ticket man and I would have expected a line up like the last time I was here."

Amy parted the curtains and waved the others over. "Straw on the floor, and ooh, what were they feeding it, rotten hay? That's a terrible smell."

Qiu Yu reached down for a scrap of paper. "Hey, look at this! It's a betting form from the race track."

"So?"

"Think. The unicorn predicted that Sorrow would find her baby at the race track. Maybe they've hidden the zhi somewhere nearby."

"Let's split up and ask around," said Amy. "Someone here must have seen it being taken away."

But ten minutes later they met back at the curtains without any more information other than the slip of paper they had already found.

"These people are hiding something. It's like they're all afraid to talk about it."

"I know what you mean, especially when I asked about the race course. There was a real fear in their eyes."

"I hadn't noticed that — very perceptive, Amy."

"I think we've started to draw too much attention to ourselves," Soo-Lin announced.

As the girls glanced around they could see several groups of men gathering together and pointing in their direction.

"There are only two ways out of here," said Sorrow. "Jump off the roof like the people who have lost everything, or go back down the stairs."

"Let's leave the roof for another time," suggested Amy, "and run. Now!"

All four girls hit the stairs flat out and bumped and jostled their way back down to the first floor. Sorrow waved good-bye as she blended into the crowd heading for the auditorium. Amy, Soo-Lin and Qiu Yu dashed out into the street, laughing with delight at their escape.

"That was exciting!" exclaimed Qiu Yu. "What should we do now?"

"I'll send word for Sorrow to meet us at the race track tomorrow afternoon," replied Amy. "We need to find out if the zhi really exists and whether its premonition will come true."

秋玉

13

Raindrops were gently falling from last night's thunderstorm.

Pitter-patter, pitter-patter, drip, drip. Silence.

Now that Jamie had returned, I figured we wouldn't have to work so hard. But, as I lay in bed, I could hear fragments of a loud argument coming from the barn.

" . . . come back?"

" . . . in too deep . . . "

" . . . Bruce . . ."

" . . . cover up . . . "

Boots stomped across the gravel and then Mrs. Davis boomed out across the yard. "What the heck is going on in here?"

The conversation became more hushed after that. I couldn't pick up anything else. I looked over at Vanessa.

She rolled over and moaned. "Did you get all that? What an awful night! I hardly slept at all once we got back."

"You're kidding! I love the sound of thunder. I feel quite refreshed."

"Breakfast should be interesting," Vanessa commented.

I parted the curtains and warm sunshine beamed into our room.

"Come on, sleepyhead!" I laughed. "Mr. Davis said we could go for a horse ride today if it was nice out — and look, it is."

We both dressed quickly and raced down the hallway to the kitchen.

A very subdued Jamie and Mr. Davis came in for breakfast. The conversation, what there was of it, was strained and quite mundane. Weather and neighbourly gossip can only go so far. It was very quiet near the end of the meal.

We followed Jamie out to the barn.

"I've heard you two have been doing a great job," he began.

"Thanks," Vanessa quietly replied.

Time to turn on the charm. "Where's Bruce?" I asked.

We had him on the defensive. "He won't be coming back. It was worse than we thought. They transported him to a hospital in Vancouver."

As he moved into the barn, I mouthed "Liar" at his back. Vanessa nodded in agreement.

The morning routine quickly lost its charm.

"Saltine isn't behaving right," I said to Vanessa. The horse was acting very restless, pawing and stamping with her hooves.

"Has she turned around and checked out her flanks?" queried Vanessa.

"Yep, and she's just done it again," I replied.

"I think she might have colic. It's sort of the same as a bellyache for us. Where did Jamie go? He should be able to tell us!"

"There's no time to look for him. You better let Mr. Davis know that Saltine's in trouble."

Vanessa ran out of the barn while I tried talking softly to Saltine. She lay down and rolled on the floor, sweating profusely.

Vanessa ran back into the barn. "They're on the way!"

"I'm getting worried. Can't we do anything to help her?"

"I've only seen colic once before and never as bad as this."

We were both reaching panic mode when Mr. Davis arrived with Jamie in tow.

"Get her up!" commanded Mr. Davis. "She needs to walk to help dispel the gas."

Once she was up, he stated more calmly, "Saltine's done this before. I'll mix up a drench for her."

Mr. Davis spooned out two heaping tablespoons of bicarbonate of soda into a jar of warm water. Jamie, Vanessa and I coaxed, pushed and prodded Saltine to stay standing. Mr. Davis opened her mouth wide and poured in the drench.

"Keep her walking. If she's not better in twenty minutes, we'll do it again. Jamie, go call the vet and let her know we might have an emergency."

"I didn't think there was a vet on Mayne Island," I said to Mr. Davis.

"You're right. She's on Saltspring. Her husband has a speedboat for getting her out to the other islands."

Saltine was slowly relaxing. Mr. Davis had given her a second bicarbonate drench, even though she already seemed to be feeling better.

We all breathed a sigh of relief. Mr. Davis had noticeably cheered up. "Thanks! I've had ranch hands that didn't act as calmly and professionally as you two." Could that comment have been directed at Jamie and Bruce?

We all returned to our chores.

After eleven-thirty I started checking my watch. If Adam was coming, he should have been here by now.

In the distance we could hear a soft 'put-putting' sound. There was also a faint aroma in the air. I was beginning to crave French fries, of all things.

"Whatever it is," I said to Vanessa, "it's coming closer."

The noise was louder and the French fry odour became very distinct. Suddenly a bicycle appeared at the end of the driveway. There was a trailer of sorts hanging off the seat post of the bike. Sitting proudly on the props for our play was Watson.

"It's Adam!" Vanessa cried out.

"This must be that big secret he's been working on all summer!" I exclaimed.

We quickly put away the grooming brushes and rushed over to greet Adam. Watson jumped off the trailer and nearly bowled me over.

"Morning, ladies," Adam boomed out, grinning from ear to ear. He pressed a switch on the handlebars and quiet filled the air. On the back of his bicycle Adam had mounted a small motor; a cylinder for the gas hung from the bike's cross bar.

"I just know you want to tell us all about it," I laughed.

"But we've got news too, so don't take all day," added Vanessa.

"Sure thing." Adam dismounted and pointed at the small motor.

"Remember that day at the beach, when I spotted something shining in the trees? I guess somebody's remote control airplane had crashed and they couldn't find it. The body of the plane was damaged and the electronics were all corroded. The motor seemed fine though, so I climbed the tree, pulled off the motor and stuffed it into my beach bag."

"Why were you mysterious that day?" Vanessa asked.

"I wanted to keep the motor, but I knew it was worth a lot of money. I felt guilty for taking it, so I didn't say anything. When I got home Mom suggested I place an ad in the local paper. When no one responded my parents said it was okay to keep it. That's when I got my bright idea . . . "

"Putting a motor on a bicycle is not much of a brainstorm,

Einstein," I mused.

"Ah, but you see Ms. Know-it-all, this isn't an ordinary motor. It's rare for model cars or airplanes to have a diesel engine, but this one is diesel and . . . " Adam paused for effect. "I made the fuel myself!"

"What!" Vanessa and I both exclaimed.

"You'd need your own oil refinery," challenged Vanessa.

"It's called biodiesel," replied Adam. "I read about it in a magazine. I did some research on the Internet and found a formula for making it. The main ingredient is discarded deep fryer oil . . . "

"The French fry smell!" I snickered.

" . . . right. You know how restaurants sometimes have a really stinky barrel of old oil sitting out back? I found a Mr. Burger that let me take as much as I wanted for free. The process is kind of dangerous if you're not careful — that's why I had the lab coat and big gloves."

I laughed, recalling the image of Adam as a mad scientist.

"So, was it easy to make?" asked Vanessa.

"That's my biodiesel in the gas tank," Adam proudly pointed. "With a bit of tinkering I now have a motorized bike that flies up the hills. It hardly uses any fuel and it only costs me pennies to run!"

"Wow, Adam, that's amazing!" I was bursting with pride for his accomplishment.

"So, what have you two been doing without me?"

Vanessa and I took turns filling him in on the mysterious submarine, the unicorn I'd seen and the strange behaviour of Mr. Terces, Bruce and Jamie.

"Don't forget the note that Mr. Davis passed to Jamie," added Vanessa.

"Any idea what was on the note?" said Adam.

I buried my head in the palms of my hands. "Oh, I'm so slow."

"Huh," said Vanessa.

I dug into my pockets. "Remember the list of chores Mr. Davis gave us? If he wrote the note to Jamie first, there might be an impression of the letters on our piece of paper! Adam, do you have a pencil?"

He began rummaging through his front pannier. "I've got one in here somewhere, ah ha!"

I gently unfolded and flattened the piece of paper. I lightly rubbed the pencil lead over the entire sheet. "We're in luck!" Words were appearing. I couldn't make out all of the letters, but there was definitely writing on the paper.

"Copy it out," urged Vanessa.

C, l, the next letters were too blurry, r, space, o,u,t, another space, t, h. I did my best to make out the rest.

"What's it say?" asked Vanessa.

I took a stab at filling in the missing characters. "Clear out the lab. Move the zhi. D."

Adam bent over laughing. "Autumn, Vanessa is right. You are a magnet for mysteries. Who else would have stumbled onto such strange things while on a simple trip to Mayne Island?"

"You laugh now, but I think these people mean business."

Watson was at the fence staring intently at the horses. "Ahem," I cleared my throat to get his attention. "Behave yourself or you're out of here."

I suddenly realized that Adam should have been here sooner. "Say, if your bike is so fast, how come it took you so long to get here?"

"The most amazing thing happened to me. There was a rock band on the ferry. When I got to Miners Bay, they were setting up to record a music video."

"Anyone we'd know?" interrupted Vanessa.

"They're called 'Idiot Savant' — I saw them last year on a cable TV show. Heard of them?"

"Nope, are they any good?" I asked.

"I like their sound . . . Anyway, I stopped to watch and the drummer let me try out his kit while they were warming up. I got to pretend I was a big rock star. And that's why I'm a little late."

I slapped my left side and Watson moved into a heel position. "Adam, let's get your stuff unpacked. Your great day hasn't ended, yet. We're going for a horse ride after lunch!"

秋玉

14

Adam was nervous: shaky legs, sweaty palms, I-don't-want-to-go nervous.

"Honestly, Adam," giggled Vanessa, "Mr. Davis promised that Rainbow was the gentlest horse he'd ever owned. You'll be fine."

"Where's Watson?" asked Adam.

"He's pouting on the front porch. I told him he couldn't come on the ride. I don't think he's very happy with me right now!"

Jamie was waiting for us in the paddock. He had Scamp, Fly and Rainbow with him.

"That little fellow is Rainbow," I pointed. "You should be fine on him."

"He still looks big enough to me," Adam shuddered.

Jamie waved Adam over. "Hey, greenhorn. I heard a rumour you've never ridden before. Is that true?"

"Afraid so," replied Adam.

"Well, come on over and I'll get you saddled up."

Adam slowly inched closer to Rainbow. The horse lazily peered down at Adam and made a soft clicking sound.

Jamie started his riding lecture. "We use an English saddle for riding instead of a Western saddle."

"Why not a Western saddle?" I asked, figuring Adam wouldn't know there was a difference.

"A Western saddle is used for a different purpose. It was designed for cowboys who spend long days riding the range, driving and working cattle."

"Do the horses like to be ridden?" asked Adam.

"Well," Jamie chuckled, "you wouldn't stay on their backs for very long if they didn't want you there."

Adam looked even more nervous.

Jamie positioned the saddle on Rainbow's back. "Vanessa, could you buckle up the girth on the other side?"

Vanessa stroked Rainbow under the neck as she moved over to the other side. Jamie held up a complicated arrangement of metal and leather. "Anybody know what this is called?"

"The bridle?" Adam guessed. I gave him a big thumbs up.

"Exactly! The bridle is used for controlling the horse. The halter goes around the neck, like this, the reins go over the head and then the bit goes in his mouth."

"Hey, wow," exclaimed Adam. "He just opened his mouth right up to take it."

"They are trained from the time they are foals to accept it. Okay, a couple of buckles to do up and you're ready to ride."

Jamie reached into a large canvas bag and pulled out a black riding hat. "This should fit you."

"No thanks," responded Adam. "I've got a baseball cap I can wear."

"Wrong!" Jamie rapped the hat with his knuckles. It made a metallic thunk. "No helmet, no riding. That's the rule around here. This will save your life if you take a fall."

Adam put on the helmet and grabbed the saddle. "Don't laugh, but how do I get on?"

"Put you left leg in the stirrup. Swing your right leg over the saddle and place it in the other stirrup."

The first time Adam didn't swing his leg high enough and he bounced right back to the ground.

"Put some effort into it," I cajoled.

"Here, let me give you a leg up," offered Jamie.

He gave Adam such a big push that Adam flew up and almost over to the other side. Luckily Vanessa helped him stop and catch his balance.

"Whew, thanks. I think the stirrups are too short," complained Adam, his knees up around his chest.

Jamie loosened a buckle. "Vanessa, you do that side and I'll adjust this one."

Adam tried to look relaxed in the saddle. "Now what? How do you drive this crazy contraption?"

"Think of the horse like it's a car," sighed Jamie. "Your legs are the gas pedal. A gentle squeeze will get Rainbow started."

"And to stop?"

"Your reins are the brakes. Pull back to slow or stop. Saddle up, girls, I think your friend is ready to ride. Don't take too long, though. You've got chores to finish."

"You choose, Vanessa," I said pointing to the two remaining horses.

Vanessa picked Fly, and that left me riding Scamp. I liked Scamp. She had always been very gentle while I was brushing her. It was just over a year since I'd last ridden a horse. "I forgot how much fun this was! It felt great to take some weight off my gimpy leg."

"You've been doing pretty well with your leg. I hadn't noticed that it was bothering you," said Vanessa.

"It comes and goes. All the work we've been doing has helped keep me limber."

Adam had slowed down as Vanessa and I were talking

"How ya' doing, pardner?" I called over to Adam.

"You okay?" asked Vanessa.

"This is hard work! I just know I'm going to be stiff and sore tomorrow."

I moved over and made room for Adam to come up between us.

Vanessa lightly bounced up and down in her saddle. "There's a trick to riding. Watch how I'm moving — it's called posting. It helps keep you relaxed and comfortable for long rides."

Adam gave it a try. Vanessa and I both started laughing. He was riding like he had a broom handle up his back.

"Relax, silly," I snickered.

"Where are we going?" asked Adam.

"Well . . . I'd really like to head up to where that creature was standing. Maybe that's where we'll find the lab from Mr. Davis' note."

"You didn't give me much detail in your email. Can you describe again what you saw?"

"It was the wailing that woke me up. The animal was too far away to see clearly, but there was a definite silhouette of a horn coming straight off its forehead."

"Why do you think it was a unicorn? Wouldn't a goat or a deer be a more likely candidate?"

"I would have said yes until last night. Tell Adam what you saw, Vanessa."

"Adam, there were two foals born last night. They said the first one was stillborn, but I think I saw it move. I only had time to get a quick glimpse of it under the tarp. There was a bump on its head like the stub of a horn, and it was like no horse I'd ever seen before.

I managed to feel its skin. It was still warm to the touch!"

"I bet you it was only drugged," suggested Adam, "and not dead like they told you."

We rode in silence for several long minutes. Vanessa stopped and pointed at a stand of trees. "There's a building in there. Can you see it?"

I strained to see. "No . . . wait. I got it. Looks old."

"Can I get off this horse and walk?" begged Adam.

"Sure, let Vanessa and me dismount first and we'll hold Rainbow steady for you."

I slid my right leg over the back of the saddle and dropped lightly to the ground. Adam's dismount was more of a plummet.

"Not bad for a first time!" I slapped him on the back.

"Yeah, right."

We left the horses tied to a fence post and continued on foot.

"Hello!" I cried out.

"Looks like no one's been here for years," commented Adam.

Vanessa peered through a dirt-stained window. "More like only a few days. There are still dishes in the sink. I bet they've made the windows dirty on purpose."

Adam tried the front door. "Locked!"

"Let's see if there's a back entrance. We can check all of the windows as we go around the building."

The first window was nailed shut. I could make out shelving with assorted glassware through the dingy glass.

Adam called us over. "I found one!"

It was a small basement window hidden behind a low bush.

"I'm too big. Vanessa or Autumn, think either of you could fit?"

Vanessa leaned on my shoulder and whispered softly in my ear. "I'm never going to squeeze my chest through that little opening."

She was right.

"I'll give it a try," I volunteered.

Adam held the window open as I squirmed my way backwards. I slowly lowered my feet, trying to get a foothold on something solid.

"I need your arm, Adam. It's too dark to see the floor. You'll have to lower me the last few feet."

Once my eyes adjusted there didn't seem to be anything interesting in the basement, just a bunch of mouldy boxes and dusty cobwebs. "Phew, it smells like rotting hay in here." The stairs to the first floor were close by. "I'll meet you at the front door," I called up to Adam.

"Be careful, you may not be alone in there," he warned.

The staircase creaked loudly as I put my weight on the bottom step. I gingerly moved up the staircase, afraid that at any minute I would fall through. It took several tries to push open the door at the top of the stairs.

I was in a lab. Well, more like a workshop. The glassware was really old preserve jars with assorted nails and screws. Bits of wire and odd-shaped pieces of wood were strewn across a long workbench.

Strange. Now that I was inside, I could see that the front door was metal. A big steel bolt and a metal padlock locked it from the inside. Someone was knocking on the other side.

"Autumn, open the door."

"I can't, Adam. It's padlocked from my side."

"What?"

"It's padlocked from my side," I repeated even louder. "I'm going to check for another way in."

"Better move fast," Vanessa called out, "there's someone coming up the hill."

No time to search! I ran back to the basement door and slid

down the stairs, using only the railing and the edge of the treads for support. I shoved an empty box against the wall and pulled myself back out through the window.

Vanessa and Adam were already on their horses. I quickly mounted Scamp and we took a trail that led into the trees.

"Better keep out of sight," suggested Adam.

"Who was it?" I panted.

"I think it was Jamie," replied Vanessa.

"He must have snuck out to follow us," said Adam.

As we came out of the trees, we circled back to head towards the ranch. If Jamie was following us, he would never suspect a thing.

"Did you see anything when you were inside?" asked Vanessa.

"It was more like somebody's old workshop than anything else." I thought over everything I had seen. "There was another metal door, I think, hidden in the basement. When I moved one of the boxes to climb out the window, I caught a glimpse of a light shining from under the door. But I didn't have time to check it out."

The ride back to the stables was very subdued after that.

秋玉

15

Mrs. Davis kindly offered to drive us, and our props, down to the hall. Adam had said he'd go with his bike and trailer, but she would hear none of that.

"There's quite a buzz over your play," Mrs. Davis commented.

"Think we'll get a good turnout?" asked Vanessa.

"Not much else to do around here at night, is there? You're guaranteed a full house on Saturday."

When we got there, Mr. Terces had already brought in the table and two chairs. He handed Vanessa the tea set. He was looking very nervous. A small trickle of perspiration kept dribbling down the back of his neck. He glanced at his watch for the umpteenth time and then announced, "I have an errand to run. If I'm not back by the time you're done, please lock the front door behind you."

I didn't even have time to tell him we were only walking through the scenes to get a feeling for the stage — thirty minutes or so would be fine. He turned abruptly and sped out the door.

Adam ran over to the nearest window to see what was going on. "There's a woman in a green car parked outside. He's getting into the passenger's side. They're driving off."

"Was she a brunette with shoulder length hair?" I asked.

"Yeah, how did you know?"

"Her name is Jeannie," volunteered Vanessa. "Mr. Terces says she's a reporter, but we don't believe him." Vanessa went over to move the table onto the stage.

"He sure is an odd fellow," commented Adam.

"He's supposedly filming a music video here this week. We haven't seen a film crew or a band, though."

"I have. Mr. Terces met the band I played with the other day."

"Idiot Savant?"

"Yes, I remember wondering what a geeky-looking guy like that would be doing with a cool band like Idiot Savant."

Vanessa was struggling with the table. "Where do you want it?" she asked

"There's a light above the front of the stage. Adam, could you work the switches? We'll put the table right under the main spot light."

Adam disappeared behind the curtain and started flipping the light switches.

"That's it!" I said.

I centred the table while Vanessa set the chairs at a forty-five-degree angle. Next came the teacups at each place setting.

I pulled our costumes out of a bag and passed them around. Adam cued the music for the intro and we were off. It took about twenty-five minutes to do the entire play.

Vanessa seemed puzzled. "Autumn, I was wondering about the baby in the play. Don't you think she should be crying?"

"I actually put that out as a question on the Sisters of China chat line. It sparked an interesting debate."

"Not everyone was in agreement, then?"

"Most of the girls felt that being separated in such a traumatic way from the birth mother would be catastrophic for a baby. It doesn't matter whether the baby was abandoned at three hours or three months, that initial loss is so devastating that many girls say they still suffer from it."

"That was my thinking, too."

I picked up the doll we were using as a prop and tossed it to Vanessa. Almost unconsciously she nestled the doll into the crook of her arm and started rocking from side to side.

"On the other hand," I laughed.

"What?"

"Look at yourself. A baby has four basic needs: feed me, change me, protect me, and hold me. Some of the girls hypothesized that as long as the baby's basic needs were being met it would suppress the loss of its birth mother and kick into survivor mode."

"The baby would tough it out and not cry?"

"Exactly!" I smiled. "But, to tell you the truth, I didn't want the baby crying in the play because it would be really annoying."

Adam parted the curtains. "If the philosophical debate is finished, can we get back to rehearsing?"

We went over a couple of rough spots and then packed up.

I put up my hand for high-fives. "Great job, you guys!"

Vanessa and Adam looked pleased as well.

"Not bad for a bunch of amateurs," Adam laughed. "Should we practise again tomorrow night?"

"I think we're ready. Vanessa and I worked on the play all last week. This was the final dress rehearsal. I'm feeling confident now about doing a fabulous performance on Saturday night."

Mr. Terces hadn't returned. We finished putting away our props and locked up as he had requested.

Mrs. Davis pulled into the parking lot to take us home. She rolled down her window. "I just saw the oddest thing! That Mr.

Terces was by the side of the road having one heck of an argument with a woman in a green car. His face was very red. When I looked back in my rear view mirror she'd pulled out and left him there!"

Vanessa, Adam and I all exchanged a conspiratorial look.

Naturally I was surprised to see Jeannie's green car already parked in the Davis' driveway.

"What's she doing here?" Vanessa blurted out.

Jeannie gave Watson a final pat and came down the porch steps to greet us. "Mind if I talk to the kids for a couple of minutes?" she asked Mrs. Davis.

"Why don't you ask them yourself? It's certainly none of my business." Mrs. Davis opened the front door. "If you guys get hungry, I've left some dessert out on the table."

We walked over to the horse paddock and leaned against the fencing. I snapped my fingers and Watson came bounding over. "Friends?" I asked him. In reply he curled up by Jeannie's feet.

"He's your dog, then? Very well behaved. I was watching him in the field yesterday doing the most remarkable things with the horses. Oh, where are my manners," she stuck out her hand, "my name is Jeannie, I'm a reporter for the Saltspring News."

Since she was being all friendly with us, I decided to go for it. "Jeannie, we already knew your name. I, I mean we, think you're with the FBI or CIA or something like that."

She hesitated for the briefest of seconds. Then she started laughing. "Oh, that's a good one. I've been called many things before, but never a spy!"

"But . . . "

"Okay, I'm not a reporter. I'll grant you that."

"Who are you then?"

"I'm a location scout for Emerald Movie Studios. I use the reporter cover to throw people off. You have no idea what some folks will do to get their house or business into a movie."

"You guys pay really good for a location shoot, don't you?" asked Adam.

"It's not just the money, they think we'll put them in the movie, too. It never works out though, so I like to just tell people I'm a reporter."

I still wasn't convinced. Time to lay all of our cards on the table. "But what about Mr. Terces? You make him really nervous. Mrs. Davis saw the two of you having an argument by the side of the road not more than twenty minutes ago."

"Xavier Terces is my younger brother. He's such a pompous idiot. He's directing a music video with his friends. He keeps hoping I'll be impressed and get him a big movie deal."

"Isn't that a gun under your jacket?" asked Vanessa.

Jeannie reached inside her coat and pulled out a digital camera. "I use it for sending location shots back to the studio. Anything else?"

"Sorry," we all apologized at the same time.

"It's an honest mistake."

"So what did you want talk to us about?" I asked.

"I wanted to warn you about my brother. He's hoping to pull some crazy stunt with a fake unicorn for the music video. Trouble seems to follow him and I figured you kids should know. Don't believe everything you see or hear if my brother is involved. Okay?"

"Sure," I slowly agreed. I was going to tell her that I'd already seen the unicorn, but it suddenly occurred to me that we should keep that tidbit of information to ourselves.

"I've got to go. I'll see you kids Saturday night. I'm looking forward to watching your play!"

秋玉

16

We huddled together in Adam's room. Watson sat on Adam's bed listening intently to the conversation.

"So, what does everybody think?" I began. "I still don't believe Jeannie is telling us the whole truth."

Adam put up his hand. "Can I be the voice of reason?"

Vanessa shrugged her shoulders and I nodded my head.

"Why would she lie to us? We're just kids who don't know anything, right?"

Adam held a straight face for three more seconds and then broke into a huge grin. "I agree with you guys. Jeannie was holding out on us! That whole story about Mr. Terces and the fake unicorn was obviously a cover up."

This was as good a time as any to make a confession. "The zhi is still on the island," I stated calmly.

"Pardon me?" said Adam.

"I can sense it. I know it isn't logical, but I've got this feeling in the back of my head and it's not going away."

We speculated for a few more minutes and then Vanessa and I got up to return to our room.

"Watson, you coming or staying with Adam?"

He covered his eyes with his front paws.

"All right, I promise you can come with me tomorrow."

Watson jumped up and licked my hand.

"Have a good sleep, Adam," I said.

"See you two in the morning."

Watson jumped up on my bed. He turned around several times and then positioned himself so he could watch what I was doing. I turned on the handheld and logged on to receive my mail.

"Hey, Vanessa, check this out!" I waved at the small screen of the handheld computer. "Mrs. Lee bought a new computer and sent me an email. I guess she's back from her trip."

"Good for her. I wish my grandmother was that cool."

"Mrs. Lee is not my grandmother . . . "

"Sorry, but you know what I mean."

I scrolled down to the next page. "It gets better. She wants to try an on-line chat session with us. She's given me her address."

"Can you do it with that little machine?"

"This 'little machine' is probably more powerful than the computers we have at school. I'm sure all I have to do is download the right chat client and we'll be in business."

Vanessa watched in awe as I searched for the software, downloaded and installed it and opened a request to Mrs. Lee's chat address.

"I'm impressed," was all Vanessa could say.

I also looked up Mrs. Chandler's chat address and asked her to join our session.

Autumn:> Mrs. Lee, I didn't expect you back so soon.

Lee:> I didn't think my friend would die before my plane landed. It was very discourteous of her.

Chandler:> Now, now, don't speak ill of the dead.

Lee:> Can too! She was always like that. If I arrived on time at a restaurant, she would already be eating. Most people wait. She didn't.

Autumn:> What are your plans then?

Lee:> Autumn, you've inspired me to write. That's why I bought this computer.

Chandler:> What's your book about?

Lee:> I thought a mystery set in 1930s Shanghai would be fun.

Autumn:> Hey!

Lee:> But Autumn's already got that covered. One of my passions is Chinese poetry. I want to create a translated collection for Autumn and her Sisters of China friends to enjoy.

Autumn:> That's cool!

Lee:> I knew you would like it. There's more to this crusty old lady than meets the eye :)

Autumn:> Didn't have to tell me that!

I could see Vanessa fidgeting beside me. "Sorry, but Mrs. Lee is very traditional when it comes to conversations. We have to pretend like everything is all rosy for the longest time before we get down to business. Mrs. Chandler understands the game of proper protocol as well."

After a polite amount of time I finally broached the subject.

Autumn:> Hey, you two, we've got ourselves a real mystery here.

Chandler:> Oh?!

Autumn:> We think there's a Chinese unicorn or zhi on the island. Do you know anything about them?

Lee:> Only the old stories that parents tell their children.

Autumn:> Such as?

Lee:> Sorry, I'd have to think hard to come up with something useful.

Autumn:> You believe this could be for real, though?

Chandler:> Let me answer that one. Anything might be possible using modern cloning techniques. There are also scarier possibilities, like gene modification and gene splicing that can entirely alter an animal.

Lee:> If someone is fooling with nature to create a zhi, then only bad will come of it.

Autumn:> I'm exhausted, time for bed. Thanks!

Lee:> Call again if you need help, this was fun.

Chandler:> Same goes for me. Take care!

I typed in zaijian to Mrs. Lee and bye to Mrs. Chandler. I was about to quit the chat program when the screen blinked twice and another conversation began filling up the screen.

"Vanessa, this is wild!"

"What is it?"

"Must be the wireless connection. Somehow my computer is picking up someone else's transmission."

"Let me see."

"It makes no sense, though."

A:> r u ready?

T:> xfer tomorrow tonight, CB

A:> same time?

T:> agreed

The screen blinked again and then went blank. I moved the handheld around in the air but whatever signal it was receiving was gone.

"Anything?" asked Vanessa.

"Nope."

Vanessa began to smile. "Could CB stand for Campbell Bay?"

"Brilliant! I bet you anything the submarine is coming back tomorrow tonight. We need to find a boat and be there to meet it."

"There's a canoe behind the barn with life jackets and paddles. We could ask Mrs. Davis if it was okay to use them. If we leave the canoe by the shore we can head down again once it gets dark."

"I like it! We'll tell Adam in the morning. I know he'll want to come along." I let out a big yawn. "It's been a long day. I'm very sleepy."

"Me too. Goodnight, Autumn."

"'Night, Vanessa. I'm just going to make a quick note in my diary and then I'll turn off the light."

Vanessa was already snoring into her pillow. I pulled out my Dear Ghost Mother Diary.

Dear Ghost Mother, where to start? Do you believe that unicorns could be real? Maybe I just have an overactive imagination (not!) and I keep seeing a mystery where there really isn't one. Talk about losing credibility if I'm wrong. It'll be back to Detective 101 for me. Hopefully tomorrow will bring some light to this puzzle. As always, your white tiger.

I turned out the light and snuggled up to Watson.

秋玉

17

Sorrow signalled to the girls from inside the entrance to the Shanghai Race Club. She was impeccably dressed, as usual, in a beautiful silk pantsuit. The three girls were excited to see if the unicorn's predictions would come true.

"I feel like a poor cousin from the countryside," Soo-Lin moaned, smoothing out her own clothes.

"You and me both," agreed Qiu Yu.

"If we find the unicorn, I'm hoping it predicts great wealth for me and my family," stated Soo-Lin.

Amy shushed the others. "Sorrow doesn't have a baby with her."

"She doesn't look disappointed, though," said Qiu Yu.

Sorrow gave each of them a brief hug. "I have the most wonderful news. The first part of the unicorn's prediction has come true!"

"Really?" asked Amy.

"But, I don't see a baby," said Soo-Lin.

Sorrow waved them towards the betting area. "Come with me." She pulled out a silk purse stuffed with a wad of paper money.

"My life's savings," she confessed. Sorrow handed it to the teller and placed her bet. "All of this on Salt 'n Pepper in the third race."

Amy was stunned, "But . . . "

"Trust me," responded Sorrow. "I have a surprise for the three of you. Let's hurry. The first race is about to start. I've reserved seats for us already."

Sorrow gracefully worked her way through the crowd. The three girls had a difficult time keeping up.

"It's like she's floating on air," grumbled Soo-Lin.

As Sorrow entered the roped off area, an elderly woman stood up and passed a bundle to her. Sorrow gave the woman a handful of coins and thanked her profusely.

Amy could barely restrain herself. "I don't believe it! It's not possible . . . "

Sorrow pulled back the cotton blanket and proudly showed off her new baby. "I was here about thirty minutes before you. I felt very foolish, but I looked behind the statue just like in the prediction. At first I didn't see the baby and almost walked away. But then it cried out and I noticed the tiny wrapped bundle hidden by an overhang. I paid the woman to watch the baby until you arrived and I could place my bet."

All three girls took turns holding the baby.

"Boy or girl?" asked Qiu Yu.

"I honestly don't know. I haven't even checked."

Soo-Lin parted the layers of clothing. "She's a girl!"

"And a beautiful one, too," cooed Amy.

Time passed quickly and the horses were lined up for the third race.

"Which one is yours?" asked Qiu Yu.

"Number eight, Salt 'n Pepper."

The starter raised his pistol. The gun fired. The horses were off.

The race was six furlongs on a sand track. Sorrow's Mongolian pony was in the middle of the front pack for most of the race. The ponies jostled for position, but there was no clear contender to catch the front-runner. In the final turn, Salt 'n Pepper's rider started to challenge the lead horses. They passed one, two horses. With Salt 'n Pepper in second place, the lead rider misjudged the final turn and hit a sun baked mud wall. Sorrow's pony easily covered the distance to the finish line.

"Whoohoo!" clapped Amy. "Go collect your winnings, Sorrow. We'll look after the baby."

Sorrow pulled out her ticket stub and held it tight to her chest. "Two down, one to go . . . "

"Two? What's the third?"

"Buying out my servitude. Once we're done here, I'm going straight to my guardian's home and pay him off."

Sorrow left to collect her money.

"We need to find that unicorn," stated Soo-Lin. "I want to be rich, too." She thought of the new life the unicorn's wealth could buy her — freedom from the Creek and comfort for her aging uncle and younger brother.

Qiu Yu touched the vials in her pocket, tracing their shapes with her finger. "When Sorrow returns we'll tell her we're going to scout around."

"I'll stay with Sorrow," offered Amy. "Somebody has to make sure she doesn't get robbed."

Soo-Lin and Qiu Yu looked at each other uncertainly.

Amy's face brightened. "Wait, there's one of the security guards from the consulate! I'll see if he can do us a favour." She handed the baby to Qiu Yu and skipped down the stairs towards a tall, muscular man.

Amy returned with the security guard just as Sorrow came

from the opposite direction. Sorrow was holding on tight to a box wrapped in red paper. Amy did the introductions. "Sorrow, this is Sergeant Nickles from the British consulate. He's kindly consented to escort you home."

The Sergeant looked pleased to be in the company of such a beautiful companion. He took the box from her. "Shall we go, Miss? I know a dependable cabbie that will get us to wherever you want to go, safe and sound." He smiled. "I might even be back in time for the sixth race."

Qiu Yu passed the baby to Sorrow and whispered, "Good luck!"

As soon as they were gone, the three girls headed down to the stables to find the unicorn.

"If it really is here, they might be disguising it as a horse," speculated Amy.

"You can't hide the horn that well," scoffed Qiu Yu. "Anyway, you're probably imagining a unicorn from European mythology. The Chinese unicorn is not even close to a horse. Auntie said it's actually closer to a small goat."

The ponies were stabled in blocks of two-story brick buildings. They were groomed and exercised by Chinese and White Russian assistant trainers. The stable area was fairly quiet since most of the horses were being warmed up for the day's races. The girls stopped at the entrance to each stall and peered inside.

As they approached the second to last stable on the first level, Qiu Yu felt a tingling sensation in the back of her head and caught her breath in excitement. "The zhi is here. I can sense it. I'm supposed to go inside — on my own."

Soo-Lin was close to tears. "It's not fair! Why did it pick you? I have nothing!"

Amy put her arm around her friend. "Soo-Lin, we should let Qiu Yu go."

Qiu Yu slipped through the stable door and squinted into the darkened room.

The zhi moved out of the shadows and lay down at her feet. Its rainbow coloured fur was dappled with grey and white. His eyes were yellowed, reminding her of an old man she'd once seen in the hospital.

"You are correct." A voice with a musical lilt shared her thoughts. "I am the last of my kind and I am dying. Calm your mind and empty it of all thought. I want to offer you one last prediction of the future before I'm gone."

Qiu Yu knelt beside the zhi and softly stroked its head, hoping her gentle touch would comfort the creature. Strange images began to form in her mind. Tall buildings that reached up to the clouds. A city by the sea, peopled by men and women representing all of humanities' various hues. A young Chinese girl wearing a jade pendant — her jade pendant! The one that she had lost when Sergei's restaurant had exploded. The picture shifted and the young girl was now in old Shanghai with her family. The picture shifted again. Qiu Yu herself was in a museum holding the same pendant in her aged and wrinkly hand. It must be in the far distant future! "The pendant is the key to a treasure of immense value," said the zhi's voice, as the images began to fade.

The zhi's breath was slowing as it reminded Qiu Yu to fill her Aunt's ceramic vials. "Like a phoenix rising from the ashes, I will die so another may live. Let me help you."

Three silver tear drops fell from the zhi's eye, and Qiu Yu caught them in the first vial. The zhi bit its tongue and several drops of bright red blood slid into the second one. Qiu Yu found a loose tuft of fur on the zhi's mane and placed it into the third vial. Then she gently closed the zhi's eyes. Qiu Yu was still sitting there when Amy and Soo-Lin quietly came up behind her.

"It's gone," she stated sadly.

"Did you . . . " began Soo-Lin.

" . . . talk to it?" interrupted Amy, so that Soo-Lin would not say anything to reveal her disappointment with the zhi choosing Qiu Yu. But Soo-Lin had already decided not to say anything to spoil Qiu Yu's happiness.

"Did you have a vision?" finished Soo-Lin glaring at her redheaded friend.

Qiu Yu smiled. "I think I have seen the far distant future. It doesn't make much sense to me right now. I saw a picture of myself as a very old lady, and I met a girl wearing my jade pendant." She gave the zhi a final hug and stood up.

Qiu Yu gently patted her jacket to make sure the three vials were safe and sound, then held out a hand to her two best friends. "Come on you two. I think I've found a way to make our fortune!"

* * *

I woke up shivering. I reached for my notebook and wrapped a blanket around my shoulders, wrote down the highlights of the dream and then went back to sleep.

秋玉

18

I was jarred into consciousness by the sound of heavy trucks on the gravel driveway beside the barn. Voices I didn't recognize were echoing around the yard. I picked up my watch. "Seven in the morning!"

"Huh?" mumbled Vanessa.

"Come on, we need to get dressed. Something big is happening out front."

We threw on our clothes and raced down the stairs. Watson straggled along behind. I put out a bowl of food for him. He slowly perked up as the noise outside registered with his still sleepy brain.

"It's a movie crew," exclaimed Vanessa.

"What a coincidence. Let's see if Mrs. Davis can tell us who they are."

Mrs. Davis was muttering to herself. "That man is so annoying," she said as she chopped a watermelon in half with a single slice of her cleaver. "Girls! I'm afraid you're on your own for breakfast. Chores too, for that matter. It's going to be busy around here today."

"This is quite a surprise," I commented.

"Yes," agreed Vanessa, "how come no one mentioned this last night?"

"Why indeed? My soon-to-be-late husband . . . " she hacked at the watermelon again, " . . . received a phone call late last night from that Terces fellow."

Vanessa and I exchanged glances.

"Seems he had a sudden brainstorm and wanted to shoot his music video here at the ranch today. A big unicorn scene, I think."

"Unicorn!" I cried out a little too loudly.

"Yeah, beats me what he's doing. Wants to dress up one of the horses as a unicorn and film it prancing around the field." Mrs. Davis did a very good impression of a unicorn prancing around the kitchen. "I don't get it, but then I hardly ever bother with movies."

A bleary-eyed Adam wandered into the kitchen and yawned for several seconds. We wolfed down our cereal and fruit as quickly as possible.

"Thanks, Mrs. Davis. We're off to see what's happening, and then get to work."

"Glad somebody has some sense in them today," she muttered.

Mr. Terces was barking orders to a leather-clad crew of grumbling workers.

"Who brought the biker gang?" said Adam.

"Must be a low budget video," said Vanessa.

We stepped around the cables, light stands and other film gear, and went into the barn. Two women were applying bits of a unicorn costume to Periwinkle.

"Pretty cheesy, if you ask me," whispered Adam.

One of the women turned to look at him. "Come back in an hour or two," she haughtily responded. "We've only applied the foundation make-up so far."

"Oooh," mouthed Vanessa once the woman had returned to her work. "Aren't we special?"

"Well guys, the horses still have to be fed and groomed. I don't see anyone else mucking out the stalls. Let's get busy."

As the day progressed, we used idle moments together to complete our plan.

"Do you want to bring Watson in the canoe?" asked Adam.

"Too dangerous, I think. It's best if we leave him here."

The film crew was still hard at work as we quit for the day. After a quick dinner we made our way behind the barn.

"It's heavy!" I groaned, grabbing one end of the canoe.

"And full of spiders, yuk," squealed Vanessa.

Adam said, "I've found a set of wheels they must use to get the canoe down to the water. We can wash all the bugs out once we get there."

Our test paddle went without a hitch. We stowed the canoe and all of the gear for our return later that night.

The canoe gracefully sliced through the gentle ocean swells. We hugged the shoreline just in case a big wave tipped us over and we had to swim for it.

Adam turned to face us. "So, tell me again why you think they'll try to move the unicorn onto the submarine tonight?"

"We're getting too close. I don't buy any of the smoke and mirror games being played on us. They've got to get the real unicorn off the island before we uncover their scheme. Don't ask me how I know, but I can still sense that it's close by."

As the canoe silently glided into Campbell Bay we could see a rubber raft putting out from shore.

"Let's sneak up behind them," Adam suggested.

As we approached the raft, we could make out three men and something large covered by a tarp. Could it be the unicorn? A couple of quick thrusts with the paddles and we were alongside the raft.

Adam swung the slungshot to connect us to the raft and accidentally sent the closest guy reeling into the water.

"Oh," he grinned sheepishly.

One of the other men appeared to be pulling something out from the inside of his jacket.

"I think he's got a gun," warned Vanessa.

I brought my walking stick around once, twice and the remaining men lay unconscious in their raft.

"They didn't see that coming," Vanessa observed. "Hey, did you hear that? I think somebody is shouting at us."

"Let's move fast. The submarine should be here any minute now. We have to get the unicorn back to shore."

An antenna appeared and then the whole conning tower pushed up right beside the canoe. The force of the water tipped up the canoe, throwing Adam over one side into the raft and Vanessa over the other side into the water.

"Quick, grab my paddle!" I shouted at her.

Vanessa got a hand onto the paddle just as a large wave picked up the whole raft and pushed us towards the shore.

"Can someone please pull me in?" Vanessa croaked, gagging on cold seawater.

"Adam, can you reach her?"

Adam bent over the side. Their fingertips were inches apart.

"On three, I'll pull on the paddle as you reach for her hand. Okay? One, two, three, pull!"

I heaved on the paddle and Adam lunged for Vanessa's outstretched hand. They locked arms and Adam grunted as he managed to bring Vanessa part way out of the water.

"Grab her other hand and help me!"

Even with the two of us pulling, it still wasn't easy. Vanessa was getting heavier by the second.

"Vanessa, hang in there, you gotta help us," I cried out.

With a slight nod of her head, Vanessa kicked herself out of the water and Adam and I finally brought her body up onto the top edge of the raft. We were almost to shore. I put my paddle into the water and gave it a couple of hard strokes.

A bright light suddenly shattered the darkness.

"Cut! Cut!" A very angry Mr. Terces was standing on the beach. "What do you kids think you're doing? I've been yelling for five minutes."

The tarp lifted to reveal two members of Idiot Savant dressed in pirate costumes. They'd wisely stayed hidden while we were making fools of ourselves.

Mr. Terces wasn't finished with us yet. "Why were you attacking everyone? You've just ruined a very expensive night's shooting!"

秋玉

19

It was Saturday morning. We were performing my play tonight, but I didn't really care. I lay in bed feeling very depressed. How could we have been so wrong? There hadn't been a real unicorn in the raft. It was just a movie prop, and a bad one, at that. The submarine turned out to be a submersible fake. Mr. Terces was furious and the actors we had hit were threatening to sue the production company and our families for damages. The whole situation had gone from really bad to completely hopeless. And yet, I still had a nagging feeling in the back of my head. Almost like last night had been an elaborate set-up.

There was a soft rapping at the door. "It's me, Adam. Can I come in?"

I got up and opened the door. Adam nervously stepped inside. "Vanessa's still asleep?"

"She's a log, don't worry about waking her. How'd you sleep?"

"Bad. I kept going over everything that's happened in my mind. I still think we're right. We've just missed something important."

"The lab," groaned Vanessa.

"Huh," I said.

Vanessa rubbed her eyes and sat up. "That old building up the hill. You saw a metal door in the basement. Remember? We have to go back and see what's inside it."

"That's going to be impossible. We can't all slip away to go searching," said Adam.

I shrugged and stretched. "You guys will have to cover for me, then, since I'm the only one who can fit through the basement window."

"When do you want to do it?" asked Vanessa.

"The sooner the better. I'll leave right after breakfast. If anybody asks, you can say I've gone off to rehearse my lines for tonight's play."

I tacked up Scamp using the same saddle, halter and reins, and we took a roundabout way out of the yard. Watson slunk along, doing his best hunting dog imitation. No one was following me — good. Without Adam to slow me down I quickly reached the stand of trees. I tied up Scamp where she wouldn't be spotted.

Adam had found a length of rope for me to bring along. I tied it to a nearby tree and fed it through the open basement window. It was much easier getting in this time.

Watson was sniffing the air and kept glancing towards the back of the building. "You stay here and stand guard. Understand?"

I quickly scooted down the rope to the basement floor. I'd brought my small flashlight and turned it on. Everything looked the same as when I'd last made my hasty exit.

I moved some boxes out of the way and tried the handle on the door. Locked. "Darn," I cursed.

It was time for my trusty Junior Locksmith kit. I pulled out the special lock picking tools and set to work.

When a voice said, "Here, let me help you with that," I almost jumped out of my skin.

"Jeannie!"

"Sorry if I startled you."

I calmed my breathing. "Sorry? I just about peed my pants. What are you doing here?"

"Same as you, I suspect. What do you think is behind door number three?"

I decided to be cagey. "We have some ideas, but they're probably all wrong. And you?"

She smiled at me. "I have my theories."

I handed her the lock picking tools. "I give up. The book that came with the kit was obviously useless."

"No promises, it's been a while." Jeannie approached the door in a way that concealed her actions. Click, click and the lock opened. Jeannie stepped into the room, pushing the door inward on well-oiled hinges.

Flash! A bright light like a camera's flash bulb went off. Jeannie jumped up and ripped something down from the ceiling. "Wireless web cam. I've just been snapped."

"Should we leave?"

"If it was being monitored, I give us two to three minutes before they're here. Let's have a quick look around. I'll set the timer on my watch so we don't overstay our visit."

Jeannie seemed way too confident. "That story about being a location scout wasn't true either, was it?"

"Nope."

"Reporter?"

"Nope."

"Can you tell me who you really are?"

"Regretfully, Autumn, it's need-to-know and you don't. If it makes you feel any better, I'm very impressed with the work you kids have been doing. We knew there was a secret lab on the

Davis' property but we didn't guess it was here."

"Right . . . " It's hard to talk to someone when they've just majorly hurt your feelings. Why didn't I need to know — wasn't I a good enough detective?

I shone my flashlight around the room. Empty! There was another door at the far end. Jeannie tried the handle and this time it wasn't locked.

"Stand back." Jeannie flung open the door and jumped out of the way. No flash. Nothing.

We both poked our heads into the doorway and waved our flashlights around the room.

"Eureka!" Jeannie was ecstatic. She flipped on the light switch by the door.

"Wow!" I exclaimed. It was a full-blown science lab, complete with fancy glassware, brightly coloured liquids, expensive computers, and wires running everywhere.

"Is the unicorn for real?" I ventured.

Jeannie was concentrating on a stack of papers. "Excuse me?"

"Is it real?"

"Is what real?"

"The unicorn!"

"I can't say."

"But I need to know! I can tell it's somewhere close by."

"You're better off if I don't tell you. This isn't a low budget outfit doing this. There is major money and heavy-duty baddies running this show. The less you know the safer you'll be."

Jeannie's watch beeped twice. "Time to go."

We closed the doors behind us. I grabbed the rope to climb back through the window.

"Come with me," offered Jeannie. "There is a back entrance that's been kindly left open."

"Argh. Thanks!"

Jeannie put a finger to her lips. "Not a word to anyone, especially your friends."

"But . . . "

"Nothing, and I mean it. You put on the play tonight. Act like everything is just peachy. I'll take care of the rest. You wouldn't want to be responsible for something bad happening to your friends, would you?"

"I'm not happy about this."

"I'm not happy that you three are involved at all. This gets more dangerous the more you know. Shake on it?"

I reluctantly shook her hand. Jeannie vanished like a ghost into the forest.

Watson came around the side of the building looking very pleased with himself. "She patted you once and you didn't think you had to warn me that she was here?"

I went to retrieve Scamp. Put on the play like nothing was happening! Easy for Jeannie to say.

When I got back, I made up a story about not being able to unlock the door. Adam gave me a long stare.

I shrugged my shoulders. "Hey, we've got a play to get ready for!"

秋玉

20

The house lights dimmed and I took a deep breath. "Break a leg!" I whispered to Vanessa. "It looks like we have a full house."

Jeannie was standing in the wings and gave me a thumbs up.

We quickly took our places on the stage. I signalled to Adam and he turned up the main spotlight. Soft Chinese music began playing in the background.

Sing Song Girls

by Autumn Parker

Characters:

Sorrow - a Chinese sing-song girl in her late teens

Amy - teenage daughter of the British Vice-Consul

Wang - Sorrow's bodyguard, late 20's

Scene: Small cafe in old Shanghai

Time: 1930s

Props: Table, two chairs, doll, tea set

The scene opens with SORROW sitting at a table, waiting for AMY. There are two chairs around a table in front of a window. SORROW sits for a period of time, fussing over something hidden inside her clothing. She seems to be very happy. AMY passes the upstage window and looks in. She catches sight of SORROW and waves. She enters. SORROW motions her over.

AMY

(as she's entering the room)

Sorrow, it's so good to see you again.

SORROW

(pouring a cup of tea)

Thank you for coming on such short notice.

AMY

(sitting down)

Anything for a friend, Sorrow. How can I help you?

SORROW

It's a very delicate matter. You must swear by your ancestors that you will use your utmost discretion before I tell you any more.

AMY

(crossing her heart)

I swear on the memory of my dear old grandmother.

SORROW

Very well, then. (reaches inside her robes and pulls out the doll, swaddled in a fleece blanket) Last night, someone left this infant at the entrance to my courtyard.

AMY

(looking shocked)

But Sorrow, why didn't you turn the baby over to the authorities? It's the proper thing to do.

SORROW

(ignores her, lifting the blanket to coo at the baby)

She's so beautiful . . .

AMY

Of course, all babies are beautiful — it's a survival thing, I think.

SORROW

(laughs)

Hah, hah. That's not the point.

AMY

What is it, then? Why would you keep her?

SORROW

I haven't told this to many people, but . . . (pauses for dramatic effect) I was abandoned when I was a baby. I spent my childhood growing up in an orphanage. When I turned twelve, I was sold to my first owner, a despicable, filthy man whom I will not even name. He lost me in a bet one night while gambling with my current owner. Mr. Hu at least has been more of a protector, providing me with singing lessons so I could earn money for him as a sing-song girl. But I still would not wish my life on anyone. That's why I can't turn this baby in. Can you understand?

AMY

Hmmm, I guess so. Can I hold her?

SORROW

(gently passes the wrapped doll to AMY)

AMY

Her features are very delicate. Look. She's squeezing my finger! (snuggles the doll in close) All right, I'll help. But you still haven't said what you need me for. I'm just a kid. I can barely take care of myself, let alone lend you a hand. Did you want me to babysit?

SORROW

Amy, I need you and your friends to help me raise enough money to buy my way out of servitude.

AMY

Is that possible?

SORROW

I have a plan – I think it's a good one too. Mr. Hu likes to gamble, especially on the horses. We're going to fix a race and he's going to lose everything to a mysterious foreigner – you!

AMY

Hold on, Sorrow. I can't bet on a horse race. Who would be dumb enough to take money from a kid?

SORROW

Trust me, and it will work. (clap hands)

WANG

(comes out and bows to SORROW and AMY)

SORROW

Wang has created a disguise for you. Pass me back the baby and then please try it on. (takes the doll from AMY and places it on her lap)

WANG

(silently lays out the clothes on the edge of the table)

AMY

(laughing)

Oh, Wang, you are very clever.

The disguise consisted of white cotton trousers, a suit jacket with a built in shirt and bow tie, a fashionable man's hat and a small moustache that matched Vanessa's hair exactly.

Adam bowed and moved off stage. He dimmed the lights, which allowed Vanessa to throw on the costume.

At Vanessa's nod, the lights came back up and now a small man appeared to be sitting at the table with me.

The audience clapped in appreciation.

SORROW

Deeper! You must talk deeper, like this: One thousand dollars on Amber Night. That's all you have to say and then pass over the money.

AMY

(with voice cracking)

One thousand dollars on Amber Night. (start giggling)

SORROW

(glares at AMY)

AMY

(trying again)

One thousand dollars on Amber Night.

SORROW

(applaud)

Better! Keep practising and you'll be fine.

AMY

(removes hat to shake out hair)

SORROW

(points at the moustache still on AMY's lip)

AMY

Oh, thanks. Now what's the rest of your plan, Sorrow? How can my betting money on a horse called Amber Night buy you your freedom?

SORROW

That's where your friends come in. We need them to spread a rumour that Amber Night is colicky but they're still going to race her. Most bets will then be placed on the number two horse in the race, Roxy.

AMY

(interrupting)

But how . . .

SORROW

Don't worry. There's more. They also need to have a conversation within earshot of my owner. They'll say that Roxy has a new rider and the smart money would bet on the third horse, Angel Feet.

AMY

(thinking about it for a moment)

Oh, I see. Mr. Hu will figure he's got the tip of a lifetime and bet big to cash in on all of the other suckers. I bet instead on Amber Night who's actually fine. She wins the race and you get a ton of money. But won't Mr. Hu be suspicious if you suddenly pay him off?

SORROW

That's the best part of the plan. A friend's uncle has offered to buy out my contract using the money I'll win. Mr. Hu will have no choice if he doesn't want to end up in the river. He will have lost a lot, and owing money isn't a smart thing, especially in Shanghai.

AMY

Assuming this actually works, where will you go?

SORROW

Wang has a sister who lives by herself in Nanjing. Life won't be easy at first, but it will be on my own terms. No one will ask me about my daughter and she can grow up loved and protected.

AMY

(sipping her tea)

When do you want us to begin?

SORROW

The next big horse race is on Wednesday. If you

start spreading the first rumour tomorrow, we can set him up on Tuesday – he's always at the same place every Tuesday afternoon.

(SORROW places the baby against her shoulder. Both girls stand up and briefly embrace)

SORROW

I will be forever indebted to you for all your kindness. Good luck! If all goes well, I'll see you at the train station next Thursday.

Adam dimmed the lights again. I placed the doll on the table and passed Vanessa my chair. She carried the two chairs off stage while Adam dashed out to help me with the table.

I did the scene at the racetrack as a pantomime. Adam announced the horse race from off stage and when he called out that Amber Night was the winner I pretended to faint.

The lights went down and it was time for the final scene. I grabbed the doll and an empty suitcase and headed back to centre stage. Adam blew on a train whistle and brought the lights back up.

Scene: train platform
Time: Thursday
Props: battered suitcase, doll

As the scene opens a voice from off-stage calls out: "All aboard!" A train whistle blows. SORROW looks around impatiently. She picks up the suitcase like she is about to leave. AMY comes running onto the stage.

AMY

(puffing)

Sorrow, I'm so sorry, I almost missed saying good-bye to you.

SORROW

Is everything okay?

AMY

I think your ex-boss Mr. Hu finally figured out what happened. It's a good thing you're leaving today. I took the long way around to make sure I wasn't followed.

SORROW

(looking worried)

AMY

It's all right, Sorrow. You have nothing to worry about. My friends are keeping an eye on him. And hey, you're free now! Can I hold the baby one last time? Have you named her yet?

SORROW

(passes AMY the baby)

(The train whistle blows again. "Final call!" is shouted from off-stage.)

SORROW

I've named her Auspicious Moon, for the night I found her.

AMY

(passes back the doll)

SORROW

(heartfelt)

May your life be full and your heart be happy, Amy. You are a friend I will never forget.

AMY

Take care! Write me through the British Consulate.

SORROW

(picks up the suitcase and moves quickly into the shadows, leaving AMY on the stage)

AMY

(wipes a tear and slowly waves goodbye)

Adam dimmed the lights and closed the curtains.

It was silent for a second, and then thunderous applause filled the hall.

Vanessa and I went back to centre stage. Adam opened the curtains just enough for us to step through. He triggered the centre spotlight for us. We both curtsied and blew kisses. What a hoot!

Vanessa and I had agreed to go back for one more curtain call, but I suddenly couldn't see her anywhere.

Adam was gesticulating wildly from behind the curtains. Once he'd closed them for the final time he came racing over.

"Mr. Terces just pointed a gun at Jeannie's head and took her out the back door. Vanessa is following them!"

秋玉

21

We left everything on the stage and took off.

"Which way?" called Adam.

"Down the street. They have to be somewhere in Miners Bay."

Adam reached the main road before me. "I thought I saw them by the Trading Post. Let's hurry!"

People were milling around outside the Hall. A little girl pointed at me. "Mommy, mommy, it's the girl from the play!"

"We better get going," I urged Adam.

I jogged as best as I could beside Adam, but my costume wouldn't let me go very fast. "Go on. I'll catch up to you."

Adam dashed ahead. I quickly pulled off the extra layer of clothes and threw them into a nearby yard. Adam disappeared around the side of the Miners Bay Trading Post. When I caught up to him, he was already crouching beneath a rear window.

Adam leaned into my ear. "I heard Vanessa's voice for an instant but it was cut short."

Somebody was pushing the buttons on a cell phone.

"We got trouble." It was Mr. Terces' voice. "My sister, who I warned you about, and those nosy kids as well. One of them followed us here. Yeah, I'm sure the other two won't be far behind."

Two sets of strong arms grabbed Adam and me by the shoulders. Jamie and Bruce! I'd guessed right that they were in on it all along.

"Come on, you two. You can join your friends."

If I'd only thought to bring my walking stick with me tonight! I'd have made mince meat of these two if I hadn't left it in our bedroom.

We were shoved roughly up the back stairs, down a short hallway and into a small storeroom. Jeannie and Vanessa were standing close together at the back of the room. Vanessa's lip was bleeding and she was acting very groggy.

Bruce pushed Adam in the back. "Watch it!" threatened Adam.

He whacked Adam on the head. "You watch it yourself, boy."

Adam clenched his fists and held his ground.

"Enough!" shouted Mr. Terces. "The submarine is on its way. Take their cell phones away and lock them in the room. We'll be long gone before anyone finds them here. Tough luck, Sis."

Bruce knocked Adam onto a packing crate and quickly retreated. "Bye-bye!"

The door was shut tight and the light turned off. We were left alone on the dark.

"Everyone all right?" asked Jeannie.

"Other than Vanessa, I guess so."

"I'm okay now," came Vanessa's voice. "Mr. Terces slapped me in the face for spitting at him."

"We need to get out of here," said Adam, pounding on the door.

"The door is reinforced steel," said Jeannie. "There's no lock to pick from the inside. We're stuck!"

Think, think. "My computer! I have it in my pocket. I guess they didn't know what it was."

"What good is that?" asked Adam.

I set it down on the floor and turned it on. Immediately the glowing red keyboard appeared and illuminated the room. "I have a wireless connection to the Internet, silly. If we're lucky, Mrs. Lee or Mrs. Chandler or even one of our friends is on-line in a chat room. We can ask them to send help!"

Adam dropped to his knees beside me. "Technology saves the day."

"Actually, it's even better than that," said Jeannie. "We've been monitoring all of the wireless Internet traffic on the island. My team should intercept your transmission and hopefully get to Campbell Bay in time to nab Mr. Terces and his entire gang."

"Your team?" asked Adam. "We've only seen you."

Jeannie chuckled. "They rented a cottage just down the road from Campbell Bay."

"You mean they pretended to be on vacation?" Vanessa asked.

"It's a great cover. No one ever suspected they were listening in."

While they'd been talking, I was searching through my buddy list. "Come on . . . "

"Anything?"

"Gotcha. Our friend Kayla is on-line. She uses the alias KoolK. I've just sent her a request for a private chat."

Within seconds Kayla's response appeared on my screen.

KoolK:> Hey, Autumn, how's it going?

JadeWarrior:> Not good. The bad guys have locked us in a storeroom

KoolK:> We?

JadeWarrior:> Adam, Vanessa, a 'reporter' friend and me

KoolK:> Is this 4 real? Are you at home having fun at my expense?

JadeWarrior:> Call my Mom if you don't believe me. In fact what I really want you to do is call Mrs. Davis where we're staying on Mayne Island

I quickly looked up the Davis' number in my contacts folder and typed it in.

KoolK:> What should I tell her?

JadeWarrior:> We're locked in a storeroom in the back of the Miners Bay Trading Post. She knows where it is

KoolK:> Anything else?

"Tell her about the sub and Campbell Bay," said Jeannie.

JadeWarrior:> Yes . . . the bad guys are hoping to escape using a submarine. They're heading to Campbell Bay right now.

KoolK:> This is exciting! Will do.

JadeWarrior:> Say hi to the rest of the gang. We'll see you all at school in two weeks.

KoolK:> Righto! KoolK out

I kept the computer turned on to help illuminate the room. "I hope your friends get the message," I said to Jeannie.

Adam was rooting around the shelves. "Cards, anyone?"

"Adam!"

"Got a better idea?"

"He's right," said Jeannie. "We might as well relax until help arrives. I know a great card game called Fifty. I'll teach you three if you'd like. Adam, can you find forty of the same thing to use as money?"

Adam dug some more and found a bag of assorted buttons at

the back of a shelf. "How's this?"

"Perfect," Jeannie replied.

Jeannie dealt out the cards as she explained the rules. Just as we completed the sixth hand the door was unlocked. It was Mr. and Mrs. Davis with Mr. Dibble right behind them!

"Everybody okay?" asked Mrs. Davis. "Strange place for a card game. You could have used our house, if you'd asked nicely."

"I feel like such a fool," admitted Mr. Davis. "I never thought it would lead to this. We needed the money to pay off a bank loan and that Terces fellow didn't ask for too much in return."

Mrs. Davis punched him in the arm.

"Ouch! What was that for?"

"Being an idiot. We should have been more suspicious when he insisted we take on Jamie and Bruce. That and wanting to borrow our old workshop for his video."

"Don't feel bad," Mr. Dibble piped up. "He had me fooled, too. I let him use one of the back rooms as his office while he was on the island."

"What about the unicorns?" I asked.

"I'm afraid there's more," Mr. Davis confessed to his wife.

Mrs. Davis looked like she was going to explode. "What!"

"They were cloning a Chinese unicorn in the old workshop. There's actually quite a fancy laboratory hidden in the basement. We were going to receive a lot of money once they were successful."

"Anything else?" Mrs. Davis asked very sweetly.

Mr. Davis hesitated, "Star wasn't really carrying twins. The other foal was their second attempt at cloning a unicorn."

"So, I did see a Chinese unicorn?" I asked.

"Don't even go there," said Mrs. Davis. "I might have to really hurt someone."

"Shouldn't we be going?" said Vanessa.

"Yeah, aren't you worried about Terces and company getting away?" asked Mr. Davis.

"My car is parked by the Agricultural Hall," said Jeannie. "We can use my satellite phone to reach my team."

I grabbed a magic marker from a box on the shelf. "Mr. Dibble, is it okay if I pay you later for this?"

"Please, it's on the house. Now go catch that so-and-so!"

We all squeezed into the Davis' car. Mrs. Davis floored it up the hill back to the Hall.

Jeannie jumped out first and grabbed the phone out of her car. She held it up to her eye for a retinal scan. The phone came alive and she punched in a long string of numbers. After a very brief conversation she hopped into her car shouting, "Follow me! You won't believe it. Watson and the horses have Terces and his gang surrounded!"

秋玉

22

What had that goofy dog been up to?

"How do you think he did it?" asked Vanessa.

"I wouldn't put it past him to have herded those poor horses across the field. He must have got some notion in that canine head of his that something was amiss."

Mrs. Davis just shook her head. "It's my fault. I took him out to the field the other day with Periwinkle and Saltine. He learned very quickly how to get the horses in a straight line."

"I always knew he was one smart dog," said Mr. Davis.

Adam and Vanessa both grinned and nodded their heads.

First Jeannie and then Mr. Davis drove right past the Davis' driveway and continued down the hill to Campbell Bay. "Good idea," said Mr. Davis. "The trail down from the road will get us there the fastest."

We scrambled down the trail. The submarine wasn't in the bay. And for that matter, neither was anyone else.

"Up here," called a deep voice.

At the edge of the Davis' property, just above the trail to the beach, was the most amazing sight. Nine full-grown horses and the colt Electric Blue were standing in a circle surrounding Mr. Terces, Jamie, Bruce and three other men. Watson was patrolling the perimeter keeping the horses in place.

"Hey, those three are the guys from Idiot Savant," said Adam, pointing to some men huddled with Bruce and Jamie. "They were really working with Mr. Terces all along."

One of Jeannie's team came over to talk to us. "That crazy dog won't let anyone get close enough to round them up," he explained.

"He's my dog," I admitted. "Let me see what I can do."

I walked over to the circle of horses, and knelt down beside him. "Watson, you need to let the bad men out. You're such a brave dog and I'm so proud of you. These other two men are on our side. They'll take it from here." I stepped back and moved my arms apart like I was parting the Red Sea.

I heard several gasps behind me as Watson swiftly moved the horses to create an opening.

Mr. Terces was the last to come out. As he reached me, he pulled out a knife with a long serrated blade. "There's nothing worse than a smart-aleck, know-it-all kid. I didn't like your type in school and I especially don't like your type now. I'm going to enjoy causing you maximum pain." He began slashing the knife back and forth near my face.

Time seemed to slow. I slipped my right hand into my pocket and pulled out the magic marker from Mr. Dibble's store. I now had something that would work with every *yawara* trick Mrs. Lee had taught me!

Mr. Terces growled and thrust his knife straight at my chest. I sidestepped slightly to the right and brought the magic marker down on his hand — hard. I then rammed the marker into his windpipe. Before the shock left his face, I tapped him on the right temple. He dropped to the ground, out cold.

Watson sniffed at Mr. Terces' head and then peed on his shirt.

"Awesome!" clapped Vanessa. "You were amazing, Autumn."

I didn't feel amazing. In fact, as the adrenaline rush subsided, I felt a sudden urge to vomit. I rushed to the edge of the field.

Adam put his arm over my shoulders and held back my hair. "Relax, kiddo. Let it all out. I'm so proud of you!"

"Adam, Mrs. Lee was right. Fighting for your life is totally different from just practising to defend yourself."

Jeannie offered me a fistful of tissues. "I'm impressed. That happened so fast none of us could help you. Where did you learn to fight like that?"

"I've got a very special teacher."

"I'd like to meet him some time."

"He's a she and she's a very cool little old lady."

"Reminds me of my favourite instructor at the academy."

"Ah, ha! I knew it."

Jeannie pulled a small leather billfold out of her jacket pocket. She flipped it open so we could read the letters inscribed on her gold shield.

"I knew it!" I gloated. "You're not a reporter, and you don't work for a movie studio."

"It was all a cover. I'm sorry we had to mislead you, but, well, this usually isn't a business for amateurs."

"I take exception to that comment." I'd already solved several mysteries and didn't consider myself an amateur!

"Hear me out, Autumn. You and your friends have proven that you're as good as the professionals. You, Vanessa and Adam figured it out. I knew my brother was in over his head but he wouldn't listen to me. Flushing out the rest of his gang took some very determined and awfully clever thinking."

"So, where does that leave me?"

Jeannie handed me a business card.

"When you graduate from college, give me a call. We need people like you and your friends to help fight the baddies of the world."

A Coast Guard hovercraft roared into the bay. Mr. Terces was still lying on the ground. Two burly officers jumped ashore. They handcuffed him and carried him back down to the ship.

Back at the road, Mr. Davis sheepishly came forward to apologize to his wife. "I'm sorry I was keeping things from you. I was promised a lot of money to stay quiet and let them use the ranch. Oh, how could I have been so stupid?"

Mrs. Davis sighed, and grabbed his arm. "Well, you were never the brightest apple in the basket," she kidded him, but then turned serious again. "I think you owe these kids an apology, too. They were in a lot of danger because of your foolishness."

I held out my hand. "Friends?"

"Friends!" he beamed. "I'll see you back at the ranch?"

"You bet," replied Vanessa. "We've got some riding to catch up on!"

I excused myself and walked over to Jeannie's car.

"Jeannie, there's one thing I still want to know . . . where's the first unicorn, the one that was being cloned? I can't sense it any more."

"Sorry," Jeannie smiled, "but the government already has possession of it. I met it this afternoon before it was taken off the island — a very interesting creature. It had a prediction for your future."

"Me?" I was taken aback. "I didn't think it would predict other people's futures, just the person it was speaking to at the time."

"Well, it did. You must have a special bond with the creature.

The vision I saw was quite clear. Very soon you will travel to Shanghai with your parents. While you're in Shanghai, you'll face the greatest challenge of your life. Oh, and your new sister will tag along and drive you crazy."

"How could she? My parents asked for a baby, not a toddler."

"I'm just telling you what the unicorn predicted."

There was something else I wanted to know. "Will I be a great detective when I grow up?"

"That is entirely up to you!" Jeannie started the car and waved as she drove off.

"But what are we supposed to do until then?" Adam laughed after I told him what Jeannie had said. "It's not like we ask for weird stuff to happen to us."

"Her advice was to just enjoy being kids while we still could."

When we got back to the Davis' house there was a message for me on the answering machine. It was my Mom in a very excited state. "Autumn, sorry to call like this, but we've just received the proposal from China. You might want to cut your trip short. There are shots to get, packing to organize. The list is endless. Dad is emailing you a picture of your new sister. She's almost four and sooo beautiful. Call when you get in. Love ya'. Bye!"

Little did I know that another exciting mystery really did await me and my new sister, in *Sisters of Shanghai.*

THE END

ABOUT THE AUTHOR

Steve Whan lives in North Vancouver, Canada with his wife, two daughters, two dogs and two cats.

The idea for the Autumn Jade Mystery Series came to Steve after the adoption of his first daughter. Steve grew up reading the Hardy Boys. That was okay for him, but where were the novels for young girls adopted from China? Steve imagined a mystery series written for his own daughter and the tens of thousands like her. Thus Autumn Jade and her world were born.

For pictures of old Shanghai and much, much more, please visit Autumn Jade at www.autumnjade.com.

Chinese Unicorn, *Zhi*
by the real Autumn Jade, age 6